Grace paused, then too⋯⋯⋯⋯⋯⋯
ago Rick was shot."

"Who shot him?" demanded Clint.

"We don't know."

"How badly is he hurt?"

"Pretty bad," she said.

"Damn it!" Clint swore. "I had a hell of a time getting here. I should have been here sooner—a lot sooner."

"You can't blame yourself," she said. "You didn't know."

"I knew that my friend asked for my help," he said. "That was enough—but my horse, and the damned railroad . . ." He trailed off, shaking his head. He finished the brandy and set the empty glass down on her desk, then stood up.

"Can you take me to him now?" he asked. "I'd like him to know I'm here."

"How long did you intend on staying in San Francisco?"

"Until I catch the sonofabitch who shot Rick. . . ."

THE GUNSMITH

266

THE RED QUEEN

J. R. ROBERTS

JOVE BOOKS, NEW YORK

This is a work of fiction. Names, characters, places, and incidents either are the product of the author's imagination or are used fictitiously, and any resemblance to actual persons living or dead, business establishments, events, or locales is entirely coincidental.

THE RED QUEEN

A Jove Book / published by arrangement with the author

PRINTING HISTORY
Jove edition / January 2004

ISBN: 0-515-13686-7

A JOVE BOOK®
Jove Books are published by The Berkley Publishing Group, a division of Penguin Group (USA) Inc., 375 Hudson Street, New York, New York 10014. JOVE and the "J" design are trademarks belonging to Penguin Group (USA) Inc.

PRINTED IN THE UNITED STATES OF AMERICA

10 9 8 7 6 5 4 3 2 1

ONE

The old boy looked as fit as ever as he cantered across the corral, ignoring Clint until he was good and ready to acknowledge his presence. Well, two could play at that game. Clint turned his back and leaned against the corral, letting his thoughts drift back to last time he'd been there, several months before . . .

Mary Giles was a buxom blonde who had caught Clint's eye immediately, and vice versa. During his latest absence from Labyrinth, Texas, a laundry had opened, giving the people in town a viable alternative to the Chinese laundry on the other side of town. Labyrinth seemed to be growing by leaps and bounds since he had chosen it years before as a place to spend his downtime.

"I'm giving some thought to moving on," Rick Hartman said, over welcome-back drinks at his saloon and gambling hall, Rick's Place.

"To where?"

"San Francisco."

"Gonna join the rich folk in Portsmouth Square?" Clint asked.

1

"Maybe just a small place," Rick said. "Labyrinth is not the little hideaway it once was."

"I noticed," Clint said. "I saw the new laundry down the street."

"You have a nose for it, don't you?"

"For what?"

"You didn't look inside?"

"Well . . . I do have some laundry from the trail."

"Take it over there and you'll see what I mean."

"Maybe I will, a little later on," Clint said. "Right now I need another of these cold, free beers."

"Free being the operative word?" Rick asked.

"That would be cold."

Rick waved to his new bartender to bring over two more beers. It seemed to Clint that every time he returned to Labyrinth, Rick had a new bartender, and a whole flock of new girls.

"You gonna go out and see the old boy?" Rick asked.

"First thing tomorrow," Clint said. "It's been a while. Maybe he won't remember me."

"I doubt that," Rick said. "You two went through a lot together."

"Have you been out there to see him?"

"Once or twice, just to be sure he was getting settled in since you moved him."

The bartender came over with the beers and set them down. It was too early for any of the girls to be working the floor.

"How's business, if you've been thinking about moving?" Clint asked. "Falling off?"

"Business is great," Rick said. "It's been growing with the town, making it take more time to run things. If I'm going to be this busy I might as well be in San Francisco. A medium-sized place there would take just as much work, and there would be more for me to do when I'm not worming."

"You finally getting bored with Labyrinth, Rick?" Clint asked. "Who am I going to talk to when I come back?"

"Come to my new place in San Francisco," Rick said. "You like the whole atmosphere around Portsmouth Square."

"Yeah, I do, sometimes," Clint said. "But I always liked how quiet this place was."

"Well, Labyrinth ain't as quiet as it used to be," Rick said. "The town council has even been thinking about replacing the sheriff's office with a legitimate police department—police chief and everything."

"Uniformed policemen walking the streets of Labyrinth?"

"See what I mean?" Rick said. "I can get that in San Francisco."

"I see what you mean. Maybe it is time for you to move on, but how about to someplace smaller?"

"Start all over again, building a new business?" Rick shook his head. "I can't do that again, I'm too old. I'd rather buy a place that's already established, and then put my own stamp on it."

"Well, I can't blame you for that. When are you leaving?"

"Hey, I said I was thinking about it."

"Don't kid me, Rick," Clint said. "You're ready. Got any potential buyers yet?"

Rick looked sheepish and said, "I've got two offers and I'm seeing another buyer later today."

"Seems like a good thing I came back when I did," Clint said. "If I'd waited any longer, you would have been long gone."

"I would have left word where I was," Rick promised. "I've worked too hard on this friendship. I wouldn't have to start another one from the beginning."

"You're a lazy man," Clint said. "You want an established business and an old friend, but in a new place."

Rick raised his beer up high and said, "All right, I'll drink to that."

They clinked glasses and drank, and then Clint pushed his chair back.

"Where are you off to?"

"Got to get my laundry done," Clint said. "I must be tired from the trail because I just realized what you were talking about."

"I knew it would come to you," Rick said. "Wait until you walk into that laundry."

Clint stood up and said, "I'll see you later tonight. I think I better take a bath before I go to the laundry."

"I think that's a good idea."

Clint turned to leave.

"Hey, Clint."

"Yeah?"

"Glad you came back when you did."

"Me, too, Rick," Clint said. "Me, too."

TWO

Rick Hartman had not yet made his move to San Francisco, but at the moment he was there looking at properties. Clint had found this out when he arrived in Labyrinth yesterday. He risked a glance over his shoulder but the old guy was still ignoring him. It had almost become a ritual they went through, and Clint just had to wait. His thoughts went back again to his previous visit, right after that bath . . .

He collected his laundry—a couple of shirts, some socks, underwear, and a pair of Levi's—and walked over to the new Labyrinth Laundry. Along the way he saw what Rick was talking about. There were other new businesses and new buildings around town. Some of the streets had even acquired extra blocks since he was last there. Labyrinth was growing up, and out.

As he approached the laundry he noticed a man coming out, and many going in. There was not a woman in sight. This reinforced his idea of what Rick had been referring to. He crossed the street and looked in the window and saw that he was right. He waited until the man inside had left, then opened the door and entered, his laundry a bundle in his arms.

The woman turned and the first thing he noticed was her body. She was full figured, wearing a cotton dress that clung to her because it was warm in the place. Her hair was almost white blonde, her eyes wide and blue, her smile broad and beautiful. But all of this he noticed—as any man would—after he noticed her body. Her breasts were heavy and round, and the rest of her was full enough to match them, but she was by no means fat.

In addition, there was a raw sexuality that radiated from her. Clint was sure it was this that started him sweating, and not the heat.

"Can I help you, sir?" she asked. She leaned her palms on the counter in front of him, a move that pressed her breasts together.

"I, uh, have some laundry that needs to be done."

"You've come to the right place, then."

Clint approached the counter and put his clothes down on it. Up close he could see very fine lines at the corners of her eyes. She had probably left thirty behind only a couple of years ago, which he liked. She was completely a woman, with no hint of little girl in her. He was past the age of wanting anything but a woman.

"Oh, these clothes have seen some hard times," she said, spreading the clothes and picking up his underwear.

"Trail clothes," he said. "I, uh, just got to town and this is my first chance to get them cleaned."

"Well, I'll see what I can do," she said, still holding his underwear. Suddenly, her nipples hardened and he could see them poking through her dress. He started to sweat even more.

She turned away, giving him a rear view that was every bit as intoxicating as the front. When she turned back she was holding a ticket with a number printed on it in red. She wrote down each article of clothing he had brought in, then looked at him and asked, "Can I have your name, please?"

"Clint Adams."

She looked up at him quickly.

"Is something wrong?" He suddenly felt like he had the upper hand in whatever was going on between them.

"I, uh, I've just heard a lot about you since I came to town."

"And when was that?"

"Only a few months ago. I just opened my business last month."

"How is it going?"

She paused in her writing, leaned her weight to one side, cocked her head that way, and said, "Not well, I'm afraid. All my customers seem to be men."

"I wonder why that is?"

She smiled and said, "Oh, I'm not dumb, Mr. Adams. I know why men come in here, and I know why women don't. I just need to find a way to bring them both in for the right reason."

"I guess that would depend on the quality of the service you supply," he said.

"Obviously," she said. "You'll be able to judge that when you get your laundry back."

"And when will that be?"

She handed him his claim ticket and said, "Would tomorrow be soon enough?"

"Tomorrow would be fine," he said. "And what's your name? In case I have to come in and ask for you."

"It's Mary," she said. "Mary Giles . . . but you won't have to ask for me. I can't afford to hire any help, at the moment, so I have to do everything myself."

"Sounds time consuming."

"It is," she said. "It doesn't leave me much time for anything else."

"No free time?"

"Very little."

He stood there a moment, staring at her and she boldly stared right back. Her tongue came out briefly to caress her full lower lip before darting back into her mouth. He saw the saliva gleaming there and had to quell the urge to lean forward and bite down on that lip, or at least lick it.

Her eyes dared him.

"Well," he said, "I guess I'll see you tomorrow, then."

"I hope so," she said. "Don't send someone else, because I'll only give the laundry back to you."

"What if I send someone with the ticket?"

"You'll just have to come back later," she said, "and get it yourself, Mr. Adams."

THREE

Clint was thinking about Mary Giles and her laundry when something nudged him from behind and he had to give up the rest of the memory. The nudge actually drove him forward a couple of steps. He righted himself and turned, found himself looking into the eyes of Duke, the big black gelding he'd put out to pasture several years ago.

"There you are, big fella," he said. "Finally decided to admit you knew I was here, huh?"

Duke's big head bobbed up and down. Clint reached out and stroked his nose, then his neck. He'd put on some weight since being put to pasture, but still looked fit.

"Have you missed being out there with me, huh?" Clint asked. "Bet you're sorry now you're a gelding. I'll bet there are a lot of little fillies around."

Duke rolled his eyes and Clint laughed. He heard someone coming up behind him and turned. It was Clancy Smith, the man who ran the ranch and looked after Duke.

"Hey, Clancy," Clint said. "He looks real good."

"He should," Clancy said. "He eats well and gets lots of exercise." The man extended his hand and Clint took it. "How are you, Clint?"

"I'm eating well," Clint said, "and getting lots of exercise."

"Glad to hear it. That new horse of yours is something to look at, isn't he?"

They both looked over to where Eclipse, Clint's black Darley Arabian, was standing.

"He's a good-looking animal, all right," Clint said.

"Is it true he was a gift from P. T. Barnum?"

"It's true."

"I envy you meeting him," Clancy said. "He sounds like . . . a strange man."

"Oh, he is that."

Clint turned his attention back to Duke. He wondered, idly, how the two horses would measure up if they were both in their prime. Even though Duke was not the specimen he once was, Clint was sure he'd give Eclipse a run for his money.

"Coming up to the house? Audrey just made a blueberry pie. It's still warm."

"That's tempting," Clint said, "but I just got in last night and I've got some people to see in town. I just wanted to get out here as soon as possible to see Duke."

"Well, he misses you from time to time," Clancy said. "I can tell when he's off his feed."

"Is that a fact? Well, that's good to know. I kinda miss him, too," Clint admitted.

"Why don't you bring Eclipse over here and see how they get along?" Clancy suggested.

"You're just looking for trouble, now," Clint said. "I wouldn't want to do that, Clancy. I don't think they'd get along all that well."

"You want to put a saddle on him and take him out?"

Clint turned to look at Duke.

"What do you think, big boy. Want to go for a ride?"

"I've got one saddle that'll fit him," Clancy said. "It's your old one. I've still got it in the barn."

Back when Clint had started riding the big Arabian he'd thought a new horse deserved a new saddle.

"Okay," Clint said, "I'll take him out."

He took Duke out for about half an hour, letting the big gelding run to his heart's content. He could feel the extra width between his legs, but the horse seemed to move well in spite of it. He gave Duke his head while he thought back to that first meeting with Mary Giles . . .

He went back the next day to claim his laundry, but Mary apologized and told him it wasn't ready yet.

"I'm so sorry, Mr. Adams," she'd said, "but I'm a little backed up. I haven't really been able to get to your laundry."

"Business got better since yesterday?"

"Yes," she said, nodding vigorously, "yes, it did."

She was wearing a different dress, but the results were the same. It was plastered to her body, outlining her big, ripe breasts and their turgid nipples.

"Well, all right," he said. "Not much I can do about it, I guess."

"I won't charge you, of course."

"That won't be necessary. I understand. I'm glad your business is improving."

"So am I."

"When should I come back?"

"I close at six," she said. "Why don't you come by about . . . ten after? I should have everything ready by then."

"Ten after six . . ."

"Right."

"All right," he said. "See you then."

He couldn't understand how business could have increased so much just since yesterday. Later, Rick would tell him that he was getting more and more dense in his old age. . . .

FOUR

Clint turned Duke around and headed back to the corral as he recalled returning to the laundry at ten after six. . . .

He knocked on the locked door and Mary Giles opened it and let him in. It was even warmer than before, but he assumed that as the day went on the heat rose in the place.

"I was just getting ready to pull the curtains," she said, her dress sticking to her amazing body. "Do you mind?"

"No, not at all."

She went to the windows and he watched as she stood on her toes to pull the curtains across. The dress adhered to her backside, clearly outlining the crease of her butt. He suddenly thought he'd been a fool for not realizing why he was there, and yet if he stepped forward now and took hold of her what would her reaction be if he was wrong?

"There," she said, turning to face him, "now no one can see inside."

A drop of perspiration rolled down her neck and into the top of her dress.

"I get very wet as the day goes by," she said, wiping

her forehead with the back of her wrist. "Does that disgust you? I mean, when a woman sweats?"

"No," he said, "why should it? I think it's . . . exciting."

"Really?" she asked. "I excite you, standing here like this?"

"If by 'like this' you mean wet enough for your dress to cling to you so that you might as well be naked, then the answer's yes."

"Then you know why I asked you to come here to-night," she said. "You felt it, too?"

"Yes," he said, "I felt it, too."

"Good," she said, "that's good, because I would hate to make a fool of myself by doing this."

She reached behind her, undid her dress, and allowed it to drop to the floor. Now she was naked, and gloriously so. Her skin was flawless, her breasts amazingly round for their size, topped by large pink nipples. The hair between her legs was golden, rather than the almost white gold of the hair on her head. In fact, in the light from her gas lamps her entire body took on a golden hue.

"You said I might as well be naked," she commented. "What do you think?"

Instead of voicing his answer he approached her, took her breasts in his hands, cupping the undersides and lifting them to his mouth so he could lick the salty sweat from her.

"Mmm," he said, first licking her and then sucking each nipple in turn.

"Oh, God," she said, "no man has ever licked the sweat from me before. You're right . . . sweat is exciting."

He slid his hands around her, down her back so that he could cup her large buttocks in his hands. He kissed her breasts, then slid his mouth down to her belly, kissing and licking lower and lower until his face was buried in her golden hair, his tongue probing her. The smell of her was intoxicating, both the scent of her sweat as well as the wetness between her legs.

"Oh, God," she gasped, grasping his head, wrapping his hair around her fingers. "Oooh, my . . . my legs . . . I can't . . . you're going to make me . . . faint . . ."

He felt her legs beginning to tremble, and her belly, and knew that in a second her legs would probably give way and she'd fall to the floor. Instead of letting that happen he stopped what he was doing, disengaging himself from her, and stood up.

She staggered back when he released her, one hand going to her hair, pushing it back from where it had fallen over her face. Her body was drenched with perspiration, now, as was his.

She reached for him, suddenly, and began tugging at his clothes, pulling off his shirt while he undid his gunbelt and let it fall to the floor. She then did his belt, opened his pants, and yanked them down to his ankles. With his boots still on it was difficult to remove them, but she was determined and went to her knees and soon he was totally naked except for his boots. His erection bobbed in front of her and she grabbed it in both hands and began to suck and lick it, moaning and groaning all the while.

If he'd had time to think about it he would have felt silly standing there clad only in his boots, but there was no time to think, now. They were simply reacting to what they felt, to what they had felt ever since the first time he'd walked into the place . . .

She returned the favor to him, cupping his buttocks, sucking him deep inside of her mouth, causing his legs to tremble as she suckled him dangerously close to an explosion . . . and then released him from her mouth.

She turned and he watched her buttocks twitch as she walked away from him. She stopped at the counter upon which he had dropped his laundry the day before, and climbed up onto it. Turning to face him, she drew her legs up so that she was open to him. It was the most erotic sight he could remember, and he'd had many experiences with many women, but none had seemed quite this wanton.

"Get those boots off and get over here," she said, touching herself, spreading her legs even wider. "I need that big monster in me, and I need it now!"

He got his boots off as quickly as he could and went to join her on the counter, hoping it would stand up to their combined weight. . . .

FIVE

Clint returned Duke to the corral and the big gelding still went ahead and had himself a run in there. It had felt good to be astride the old gelding again.

He walked back to the barn to drop off the saddle and looked over at Eclipse when he came out. The big Darley Arabian looked away.

"You can't be jealous of ol' Duke," he scolded the horse. "He and I have been through hell and back several times."

Eclipse refused to look at him.

"Well then, you'll just have to get used to it, I guess," Clint said.

He walked to the house to tell Clancy he was back, and to have some of Audrey's blueberry pie. After that he'd go into town and see if Mary Giles was still running the laundry. . . .

After that night in the laundry, with Clint and Mary testing the resolve of her counter several times, Clint had been with Mary a few more nights, but in his hotel rather than the hot confines of the laundry. They still managed to work each other into a lather.

When he left Labyrinth that time it was with clean clothes and erotic, dirty memories of a woman who would do anything when it came to sex. He had not encountered another woman like her in the months since then and he was anxious to see her again.

When he rode into town he changed his mind and decided to go into Rick's Place for a beer, first. As he walked in he was surprised at how empty the place felt, knowing that Rick wasn't there.

He walked to the bar where he found another new bartender behind the bar. This one looked like he'd had a career as a fighter, at one time. He had a large gut now, but still had big forearms and hands, and his nose had been broken many times.

"What can I get ya?" the man asked. Sounded as if he had been punched in the throat a few times, as well.

"Cold beer."

"Comin' up."

The bartender drew the beer and placed it in front of Clint. He picked it up, took a big swallow, then turned to look at the place. There were only about half a dozen patrons there, but that had nothing to do with how empty it felt.

"Place feels different without Rick here," he commented to the bartender.

"You know Mr. Hartman?"

"Yes, we're good friends," Clint said. "It's not like him to not be here when I come to town, but I happen to know he's in San Francisco, at the moment."

"Yeah, he is," the barman said. "I guess maybe you do know him."

"Yeah, I do."

The man put his bar rag down and squinted at Clint.

"Are you Clint Adams?"

"That's right."

"I thought so."

"Why?"

"Ain't nobody else would know where he went."

"What's your name?"

"Barney."

"How long have you worked here, Barney?"

"Couple of months, is all . . . maybe three."

He must have gotten hired soon after Clint had left the last time.

"Hey, I got somethin' for you," Barney said.

"For me?" Clint asked.

"A telegram." Barney reached under the bar and came out with it. It was in a sealed, yellow envelope that had gotten beer spilled on it more than once. Clint hoped it was still legible.

He finished his beer and said, "Give me one more, Barney, will you?"

"Sure thing, Mr. Adams," Barney said, drawing a new one. "On the house."

"Thanks."

Clint took the beer and the telegram to a table and sat down. He took a small sip from the beer, then opened the envelope. The beer had soaked through to the inside, but the message was still clear.

The message was from Rick, and the telegram had been sent two weeks earlier.

CLINT
   HOPE THIS FINDS YOU IN LABYRINTH SOON. I
COULD USE SOME HELP, SOON AS YOU CAN MAKE IT.
COME TO THE RED QUEEN HOTEL JUST OFF OF
PORTSMOUTH SQUARE.
                                            RICK

He refolded the telegram and drank his beer. Looked like he wasn't going to have much time to spend with

Mary. He'd be heading for San Francisco the next morning. He couldn't recall ever having received a call for help from Rick before. Many times calls had come to him through Rick, but never from him.

"Barney," he said, approaching the bar.

"Yeah?"

"Did Rick go to San Francisco alone?"

"Yes, sir, he did."

"This the first telegram from him, to anyone?"

"Yep. Is there a problem?"

"Apparently he needs some help, and this telegram came two weeks ago."

"Gee, I hope he ain't in trouble."

"I'll let you know when I find out. By the way, is the laundry still open down the street?"

"Oh, yeah."

"Still being run by the blonde woman who was running it last time I was here?"

"Well, I don't know who was running it when you were here, but there's this big blonde over there now named Mary—"

"Okay," Clint said, "that's what I wanted to know. Thanks."

"You gonna be in town long, Mr. Adams?"

"Just long enough to send a telegram to San Francisco," Clint said, "and to get a good night's sleep. I'll be heading out in the morning."

"You tell Mr. Hartman when you see him that if he needs more help he should send for Barney."

"I'll tell him, Barney," Clint said. "I'm sure he'll be real grateful."

He left Rick's Place, first to go to the telegraph office to send a telegram to the Red Queen Hotel, and then over to the laundry.

SIX

As Clint approached the laundry he found himself feeling wistful. He remembered the three days he'd spent with Mary last time he was in town, and was already wistful about having only one night to spend with her this time.

When he entered he immediately saw that things had changed since he was last there. Mary had three customers standing with arms full of clothes, and they were all women. When she saw Clint she grinned from ear to ear and waved to him. He waved back, recognizing that he'd have to wait until her customers left before they could talk.

"No laundry this time?" she asked, after the last one had gone.

He came up to the counter and she reached across to grab him and kiss him. The smell of her perspiration made him immediately ready for action—and the feel of her soft lips and warm tongue helped, too.

"How long do we have this time, Mr. Adams?" she asked.

"Just the rest of today and tonight, I'm afraid," he said. "I have to leave in the morning."

She pouted and he bit her lower lip.

"Well," she said, "if that's all the time we have I better close up for the day. Would you get the curtains?"

They used the counter just once for old times' sake, then moved to Clint's hotel room for a proper hello.

"I guess business has picked up," he said when they took a break to catch their breath. "You seem to have some female customers."

"Yes, the women in town finally came around."

"And apparently most of them, if you can afford to close in the middle of the day."

"Well," she said, running her hand down over his belly, "it was a special occasion, wouldn't you say?"

"Definitely," he said, as her fingers got tangled in his pubic hair, "and it's getting more special by the moment."

He'd been only semi-erect when her hand had started its trek south, but by the time she took hold of him he was hard and ready. She slid down beneath the sheets and before long her hot mouth engulfed him. She worked up and down his shaft until he was good and wet, then slid up and impaled herself. Her breasts hung down into his face and he was amazed to find that they may have gotten bigger since he was last there. They were still smooth and warm, the nipples still incredibly large and sensitive. She might have been looking at a future of being overweight when she reached her forties, but for the moment she was every man's erotic dream of what a woman should be like in bed. . . .

"Where are you heading tomorrow in such a hurry?" she asked, later. Her head was on his shoulder and their legs were tangled beneath the sheets.

"California," he said. "I got a telegram from Rick that he's there and needs help."

"I hope it's nothing serious," she said.

"I don't know," he answered. "I sent him a telegram but I haven't gotten an answer yet."

"Maybe you did but the desk clerk doesn't want to disturb us," she said. "If I remember correctly you almost had my dress off in the lobby and he got quite an eyeful."

"You know, you're right."

Gently he disentangled himself from her and sat up.

"Where are you going?"

"I want to check with the clerk and see if a reply came in."

"Now?"

"I'll be right back," he promised. "Besides, I need to stretch and take a short break."

She propped herself up on an elbow, one breast hanging slightly and the other bulging beneath her weight, and said, "Well, you better be well rested by the time you get back, Mister."

Clint left the room, wondering if he'd be able to make it through the rest of the evening and the night ahead without having a heart attack.

He went down to the lobby wearing only his jeans and an open shirt. As an afterthought he took his gun from his holster and tucked it into his waist. The last thing he needed was to be caught without it, getting himself shot with his boots off.

Downstairs he approached the desk and the young clerk smirked at him.

"Wipe the smirk off your face, son."

"Yes, sir."

"I'm waiting for a reply to a telegram I sent," he said. "Did anything come in while I was . . . busy?"

"No, sir," the clerk said. "If it had I would have brought it right up."

"Uh-huh," Clint said. "Well, keep your eyes open and

if the answer does come make sure you do bring it right up."

"Okay, sir, as long as I won't be interrupting anything."

"You will," Clint said, "but bring it up anyway."

SEVEN

In the morning Mary Giles did everything she could think of to persuade Clint to stay in Labyrinth at least one more day.

"I can't do it," Clint gasped, as she looked up at him from between his legs, his erect and pulsating penis trapped between her big, beautiful breasts.

"Are you sure?" She rolled his penis between her breasts and then stuck out her tongue to lick the bulging head.

"Oh God," he said, "I wish I could, Mary, but I can't . . . you're killing me."

"Well," she said, "you could have said yes just to get me to finish you off, and then left anyway, so I think you deserve a reward."

With that she released his straining erection from between her breasts but immediately caught it in her mouth and began sucking him ferociously. She encircled the base of his cock with one hand while her head worked up and down. She sucked him quickly, then slowed down and took him into her mouth in long, slow strokes, then increased the tempo again. When he lifted his butt off the bed in anticipation she immediately slid her hands beneath him and continued to suck him until he finally exploded into her avid mouth. . . .

They both dressed and then kissed long and hard before leaving the room together. They went down to the lobby where Clint checked out and asked again about the telegram.

"Nothing came, Mr. Adams," the clerk said. "I woulda brought it up to you."

"Okay, thanks."

Clint and Mary walked outside together and stopped in front of the hotel.

"I've got to go and open for business and try to explain to people why their laundry isn't ready, or I'd walk you to the livery stable," she explained.

"That's okay," he said. "We can say good-bye here."

"I think we spent all night saying good-bye."

"I thought that was hello."

"Well," she said, "I guess it was a little bit of both."

They kissed again briefly, and she said, "I hope Rick isn't in too much trouble in San Francisco, Clint, and I hope you both come back here real soon."

"I hope so too, Mary."

He watched her walk down the street for a few moments, then turned and headed for the livery stable.

When he got to the stable the liveryman was waiting out front. This stable was the one he usually left his horse in when he came to Labyrinth, but this time it was being run by someone new, and it was also twice the size it used to be, and there was still some work being done on it. Even now he could hear hammering from the back.

"I need my horse," he told the man.

"Uh, Mr. Adams, sir," the man said, "I want you to know it wasn't my fault."

"What wasn't your fault?"

"Those damn carpenters left some nails around on the ground and he just stepped on one—"

"What? Where's my horse?"

"He's in his stall," the liveryman said. "It was an accident, sir—"

Clint brushed past the man and rushed to Eclipse's stall. He backed the horse out and saw that he was favoring his left front hoof. He lifted the foot to take a look. The Darkley Arabian had indeed stepped on a nail, which had been removed, but it had left behind a filling there that was hot, and gilled with blood.

"That's got to be drained," Clint said.

"I know, sir," the man said. "We have a good vet in town—"

Clint turned on him and said, "Do you know Clancy Smith?"

"Sure I do," the man said. "He's a damned good horseman—"

"You go out and get him," Clint said. "I want him to take care of my horse."

The liveryman, only about twenty-four or -five, said, "Mister, if I leave I could get fired—"

"You want to live long enough to get fired?" Clint asked.

The man swallowed and nodded, his eyes bugging out.

"Then you get on a horse, or you run out to Clancy Brown's ranch and you bring him back."

"What if he can't come with me?" the man asked. "What if he ain't there?"

"What's your name?"

"Sammy, sir."

"Sammy, you better pray he is there," Clint said. "You understand? If you don't bring him back here, don't even come back yourself."

"Y-yes, sir."

"Then move!"

Clint turned his back and lifted Eclipse's foot to take another look. It wasn't a serious injury—not if it was properly treated right away—but there was no way he was going to be able to ride him for a while.

EIGHT

Clint waited outside the livery with his rifle and saddle-bags while Clancy Smith worked on Eclipse. When the man came out he was wiping his hands on a cloth.

"How is he?" Clint asked.

"I drained the wound and I don't think it will get infected," Clancy said, "but you're not going to be able to ride him for a while, Clint."

"I have to leave town, Clancy," Clint said. "I'm going to San Francisco."

"What's there that you need to leave in such a hurry?"

"I got a telegram from Rick. He needs help."

"Serious?"

"I won't know until I get there."

"Well, get another horse from the livery," Clancy said. "They shouldn't charge you, since Eclipse got hurt while in their care."

"I'm not worried about the money," Clint said. "Look, I want you to take Eclipse out to your ranch, so he can recover there."

"I can do that," Clancy said. "I'll be happy to, I just won't put him in the same corral as Duke."

"That's a good idea."

"I'll tie him to the back of my buckboard. Walking out there shouldn't do too much damage."

"Thanks," Clint said, "thanks a lot. Who owns the livery now?"

"A man named McGinnis."

"What's he like?"

"I don't like doing business with him," Clancy said, "but that's because he's a shrewd businessman."

"Okay," Clint said, "I guess I can deal with that. I'll just have to find him."

"Sammy can get him for you," Clancy said. "Help me get Eclipse tied to the back of my wagon."

They found Sammy and sent him in search of McGinnis, and then went back inside to get Eclipse.

Clancy had left with the Arabian by the time Sammy returned with Art McGinnis, a barrel-chested man in his late forties.

"Mr. Adams," McGinnis started out, "I'm real sorry about your horse. It was them damned carpenters—"

"I don't care who's fault it was," Clint said. "I need another horse and quick."

"I wish I could help you, but I got nothing, right now," McGinnis said.

"You don't have one horse?"

"With all this work bein' done on the place I moved my stock to a friend's ranch."

"Well, where is that?"

As it turned out this friend's ranch was three times the distance of Clancy Smith's place.

"I'd give you the horse for nothing, if you want to go out there and pick one out."

"That'll take hours," Clint said. "I've got to get out of town soon."

"Well, you could take the stage."

"When's the next one leave?"

The man consulted his watch, then gave Clint a mournful look and said, "Not for four hours, yet."

"Goddamnit!"

"I got a nag you can hitch to a buckboard if you want to drive it out to—"

"I'll take the buckboard," Clint said, "but I'll go out to Clancy's place and see if he has a horse for me."

"Sammy, hitch old Beulah up for Mr. Adams."

"Right away, boss."

Clint waited impatiently for the buckboard. He couldn't believe how much trouble he was having getting out of town the first time Rick Hartman ever sent him a message asking for help.

When he drove the buckboard up to Clancy Smith's the man came out with a confused frown on his face. A few of his men stopped their work to watch Clint drive the buckboard nag by. Clint was fuming, because he was used to having men admire his animals.

"What happened, Clint?"

Clint stepped down from the buckboard and faced Clancy.

"Goddamn McGinnis had no horses because he's having work done on his stable," Clint said. "Clancy, I need a horse."

"Jesus, Clint, I'd like to help you, but I can't."

Clint looked over at Clancy's main corral, which had about thirty horses in it.

"What's wrong with one of those?" he demanded.

"I got a contract with the army, Clint," Clancy said. "You know that. It's why I can keep Duke here for free. They're coming to pick up those horses tomorrow."

"They're going to miss one?"

"If they don't get thirty on the nose the deal is off," Clancy said. "I'll be in breach of my contract."

"Damn it!"

"I wish I could help—"

"Okay, okay," Clint said impatiently, "I understand." He paused to catch his breath. He did not want to be irritated or impatient with his friend. "Do you think one of your men will sell or rent me his horse?"

"You know how hands are with their horses, Clint," Clancy said. "You could ask them, but I might have a better idea for you."

"What's that?"

"I got one more horse on the grounds you could take."

"Is it a good animal?"

"The best."

"Whose is it?" Clint asked. "Will he rent it to me? Or sell it? Whose is it?"

"Well," Clancy said, "I believe he's yours."

"Mine? Oh, wait—" Clint turned and looked at the other corral, where Duke was.

"You rode him yesterday," Clancy said. "What do you think?"

On his worst day Duke would have been a better horse than any of the thirty in the main corral, but he'd been out to pasture for a while, now.

"Clancy," Clint said, "I'm going to San Francisco."

"So what? Most of the trip will be done by train anyway, won't it?" Clancy asked.

"That's true."

"He's probably still the best horse on the ranch, Clint," Clancy said. "Give the old boy a chance."

Clint looked at his saddle in the buckboard. "Will you hold onto my saddle for me? If I'm going to ride my old horse I might as well do it with his saddle."

Clancy looked over at Duke and said, "The old guy's gonna love it."

NINE

Rick Hartman came down from his room in the Red Queen Hotel and paused on the stairs to look down at the lobby. This was the kind of hotel and casino he wanted to own. It wasn't right in Portsmouth Square with the big boys, but it was walking distance, close enough to suit him.

He came down the rest of the way and walked into the dining room. His deal included all the staff, especially the cook, and he was glad of that as he inhaled the aroma coming from the kitchen.

Of course, the deal hadn't been made yet. There were some other buyers interested, and they were all staying in the hotel the way Rick was. They were also still working on their deals with the present owner, a woman named Grace Morgan. Of course, none of the other buyers—three other men—had just left Grace in their bed after a long night of sex, and more sex.

There was a spark between Rick and Grace right at the first moment they met, but even after they had gone to bed together the first time, Grace told him it would not affect her decision. Selling her hotel was business and she was a businesswoman. She was going to make the best

33

deal she possibly could, regardless of who she was sleeping with. Rick told her she understood, but he couldn't help feeling he had a small edge over the other men.

At least, he didn't think she was sleeping with any of them.

He sat at a table he had staked out for himself when he first got there and the waiter came over to take his order.

"Steak and eggs, as usual, Lenny."

"Comin' up, Mr. Hartman."

Lenny poured him some coffee before heading for the kitchen to put in his order. It was early, but early was breakfast time for most of the people in San Francisco and the dining room was doing a brisk business.

Rick sat back with his coffee and wondered if Clint had gotten his telegram, yet. He'd sent it about two weeks ago, taking a chance by sending it to Labyrinth. He thought he knew his friend, and felt that Clint would be needing some time off from the trail pretty soon. If he was lucky he'd get the telegram and respond quickly with one of his own.

Rick wanted the Red Queen and he wanted it badly, but it was a hot property and he felt that one or two of the other buyers would not be above trying something desperate to get it. He needed someone to watch his back, and the only man he'd trust with that job was Clint Adams. He had a gun in a shoulder rig under his arm and he knew how to use it, but he was a gambler first, and then a businessman. He knew how to use the gun, but he was by no means a gunman. And since he'd spent most of the past ten years or so in Labyrinth, Texas, he did not have a host of friends in San Francisco. If he'd known that Bat Masterson or Luke Short or someone of that stature was in town he certainly would have approached them, but there was a dearth of big money poker games in the square at the moment, and men like that were just not around.

In the end he just decided to take a chance, send the telegram, and hope he got lucky enough to find Clint Adams in Labyrinth.

Lenny came with his steak and eggs and he put his thoughts aside to give his full attention to his breakfast.

Across the dining room two men sat, also enjoying breakfast of steak and eggs, but they were also keeping an eye on Rick Hartman.

"You think the boss knows?" Ed Duffy asked.

"Knows what?" his partner, Marty Breck, asked.

"That Hartman is pokin' Grace Morgan."

"Of course he knows," Breck said. "Why do you think he sent for us?"

"So when do we do it?"

"As soon as he makes up his mind and gives us the word," Breck said.

"But he's an easy target—"

"Ed."

"Yeah?"

"Stop askin' questions and eat your breakfast. I'll let you know when we get the word."

"Wouldn't mind a little of that, myself," Duffy mumbled.

"A little of what?"

"That Morgan gal," Duffy said. "That red hair, and all."

"Damn it, Duffy," Breck said, "just shut up."

Grace Morgan got dressed, left Rick Hartman's room, and moved quickly down the hall to her own. She didn't want anyone seeing her in the disheveled condition she was in. When she got to her room her black servant girl, Iris, was there waiting for her.

"Draw my bath, Iris," she said.

"Yes, ma'am."

All the rooms had bath facilities in the rooms, but none as elaborate as the one in Grace's suite. When the bath was ready Grace stripped naked and slid into the porcelain tub she had brought up from Los Angeles. Iris left the room, but would not go far in case her mistress called for her.

Grace sank down into the hot water and rubbed herself between her legs, where she was worn out from the all-night activity she'd indulged in with Rick Hartman. She was sore, but pleasantly so. In fact, touching herself felt so nice she took her hand away and stopped.

As much as she liked Rick and enjoyed sleeping with him, she was going to stick to what she had told him and not let their relationship affect her decision. Business was business, she thought, as she absently soaped her hands and ran them over her high breasts.

She knew she was taking a chance holding off on the sale. Like Rick, she felt that one of the other buyers might try something desperate, even violent, to get rid of the other buyers. Or they might simply see Rick as the biggest competition, and try to hurt him. She could have headed off this possibility by closing the sale out and picking a buyer, but that would not have been in her best interests. No, she had to look out for herself, as she had been doing for most of her thirty-eight years.

It was a good thing Rick had sent for his friend. If anything happened to him she'd feel terrible—but apparently not terrible enough to pick a buyer, yet. There was still some negotiating to be done. She liked Rick Hartman, but she wasn't in love with him. In fact, the only relationship they really had was a sexual one. He was a businessman himself, and he understood.

She used a cloth to run up and down her long, smooth legs, and then she washed herself down there again. The hot water made her close her eyes and she imagined that it was Rick's hand down there, or his tongue, and when she felt herself rushing toward a climax she quickly snatched her hand away and decided it was time to get out of the tub and get on with the day's negotiations. She had meetings set up with all four buyers today, so she couldn't be lounging around her suite, pleasuring herself—especially not when a man had already spent all night doing it for her.

TEN

Clint continued to encounter trouble getting to San Francisco to come to Rick's aid. Riding Duke was no problem. He and Duke fell right back into old patterns, and except for the fact that Duke couldn't go as long or as far in one day as he used to, riding the big gelding again was the best part of the trip.

There were two problems with the railroad. First, there was a problem with one of the cars that held up the trip, and then along the way there was trouble with the tracks that took a few days to get fixed, leaving Clint stranded in a small Utah town.

So when Clint stepped off the train in San Francisco it was almost two weeks since he'd gotten Rick's telegram. He wouldn't have been concerned if it were not for the fact that Rick had never replied to his telegram, sent to the Red Queen Hotel.

He walked back to the stock car and supervised Duke's unloading, then took the big gelding in hand, walking him out to the street in front of the railway station before mounting up.

The route from the railroad to Portsmouth Square was a familiar one to Clint and under other circumstances

39

would have been enjoyable. At the end of the trip were all of the casinos and hotels that made up the Square, and he always felt excited the closer he got to them, especially if there was a big poker game waiting for him.

But that wasn't the case now. No poker game and no gambling. Just looking for Rick Hartman to offer his help—finally.

When Clint reached the Red Queen Hotel he dismounted and stood there for a moment, admiring the facade. Over the doorway was a huge playing card, the queen of diamonds. He wondered why the place had not been named after that specific card. Then he realized that this was the entrance to the hotel. Further down the street was another entrance that led directly to the casino, and over that doorway was a huge queen of hearts.

He tied Duke off to a hitching post and mounted the boardwalk in front of the hotel. He left his rifle and saddlebags on the saddle, as he wasn't sure whether he'd be staying here or not.

The lobby was posh, a smaller version of the large Portsmouth Square hotels, all dark wood, red brocade, and silver and gold. It was nearing three o'clock, but people must have either been in their rooms or in the casino. He knew very well that when the sun went down, everyone in the area would gravitate toward Portsmouth Square, but some of them would find their way to some of the smaller establishments, like the Red Queen.

He approached the front desk and faced the well-dressed young desk clerk, who greeted him with a smile.

"Welcome to the Red Queen, sir," the man said happily. "Can I help you?"

"You look like a man who's happy with his job."

"Oh, I am, sir," the man said. "It's my pleasure to make people comfortable in our rooms."

"And take people's money in the casino."

"Oh no," the man said. "I work in the hotel, not the casino. I have nothing to do with that. In fact, I don't even gamble."

"Really. Well, maybe you can help me anyway."

"I'd be happy to."

"I'm looking for a friend of mine named Rick Hartman," Clint said. "He sent me a telegram from here a couple of weeks ago."

The man swallowed hard and asked, "Mr. Hartman?"

"That's right."

"Send you a telegram?"

"Right again."

"From here?"

"Have you got any more questions before you give me an answer?" Clint asked.

"Just one, sir," the man said. He swallowed once again before continuing. "Are you Mr. Adams?"

"That's right. So you've been expecting me?"

"Well . . . sort of."

"What's your name?"

"Benjamin, sir."

"What does 'sort of' mean, Benjamin?"

"Well . . . it means I'm supposed to let Miss Morgan know when you arrive."

"Who is Miss Morgan?"

"Grace Morgan, she owns the Red Queen."

"And was she negotiating with Mr. Hartman to sell him the hotel and casino?"

"She was negotiating with him and three other gentlemen."

"I see. Well, where's Miss Morgan, then? I guess she's the only one who's going to give me a straight answer."

"If you'll wait here I'll go and get her. I believe she's in the casino, getting set up for the evening."

"Okay, then," Clint said. "I'll wait right here."

"I won't be long," Benjamin said. "I can't be away

from my post, someone might need a room."

"Don't worry," Clint said, "if someone comes in I'll feed them the same line of horse shit you fed me."

"Thank you, sir," Benjamin said.

ELEVEN

When Benjamin reappeared he was followed by a tall, stunning red-haired, high-breasted woman in her late thirties he assumed to be Grace Morgan. Negotiating the sale of the hotel with her must not have been what Rick needed help with.

"Mr. Adams?"

"That's right," he said. "Clint Adams. And you are Miss Morgan?"

"Grace Morgan," she said, shaking his hand firmly. "I own and operate the Red Queen."

"I'd venture to say you do more than that."

"Excuse me."

"It looks to me like you are the Red Queen." Although she was wearing a green dress—not flashy but suitable for evening wear—her hair was fiery red.

"You mean my hair," she said. "Funny, but I never thought of that when I named the place."

"Ironic," he said. "Can you tell me, Miss Morgan, where Rick Hartman is?"

"Yes, Mr. Adams, I can," she said. "But you're not going to like it. May I invite you into my office for some brandy? We can talk there in private."

"Very well," he said. "It seems like the only way I'm going to get some straight answers."

"This way, please," she said, leading him behind the desk and through a curtained doorway into a long hallway. She spoke to him over her smooth, bare shoulders. "You'll have to forgive Benjamin, but I instructed him not to tell you anything."

"I see. Any particular reason for that?"

"I wanted to be the one to tell you."

"Tell me what?"

She kept walking and did not reply. Impatiently, he grabbed her arm and forcefully turned her to face him.

"Miss Morgan, if Rick is dead, tell me now and stop beating around the bush. I've had friends get killed before—"

"He's not dead," she said, and Clint felt instant relief. "He is hurt, however."

"How badly?" he asked. "What happened?"

"Could we please talk in my office? It's just down there."

Suddenly, he was aware that he was still holding her arm in a very tight grip. He released her immediately.

"I'm sorry," he said. "I didn't mean to hurt you."

"You didn't," she said, and then added, "much."

Moments later they were in her office, each with a glass of brandy. She was seated behind her desk, and he was in front of it.

"I think I've been pretty patient, Miss Morgan."

"Grace, please," she said, "and yes, you have been extremely patient." She paused, then took a deep breath. "Several nights ago Rick was shot."

"Who shot him?"

"We don't know."

"How badly is he hurt?"

"Pretty bad," she said. "The doctor is a friend of mine. Rick got the very best care, and while it didn't look like he was going to make it, he pulled through."

"Where is he?"

"In a hospital not far from here," she said. "I'll take you there in a moment. Mr. Adams, Rick and I had become fairly . . . close since he arrived here. I was aware when he sent you the telegram, asking you to come here and help him."

"Then you know why he needed help?"

"Yes," she said, "he was afraid that one of the other buyers was going to do something drastic—violent—to try and get this hotel from me."

"Steal it, you mean?"

"No," she said, "eliminate the main competition."

"That being Rick?"

"Yes."

"And so he did," Clint said, "or at least tried to. Which potential buyer did he suspect?"

"All of them," she said. "I expect he was asking you here to watch his back."

"Damn it!" he swore. "I had a hell of a time getting here. I should have been here sooner—a lot sooner!"

"You can't blame yourself," she said. "You didn't know."

"I knew that my friend asked for my help," he said. "That was enough—but my horse, and the damned railroad . . ." He trailed off, shaking his head. He finished the brandy and set the empty glass down on her desk, then stood up.

"Can you take me to him now?" he asked. "I'd like him to know I'm here."

She stood up and said, "I can already see why Rick spoke very highly of you, Mr. Adams."

"Oh hell," he said, "I'm going to be around here for a

while, so you might as well get used to calling me Clint."

"Well, Clint, you can have a room here, of course, but how long did you intend on staying in San Francisco?"

"Until I catch the sonofabitch who shot Rick."

TWELVE

The hospital was called Assumption Hospital, and Clint realized that in all the years that he and Rick had been friends he didn't know if Rick was Catholic or not.

"I know Rick's not Catholic," Grace said, "but this is where my friend works, and it was the closest to the hotel."

"You did the right thing, obviously," he said. "More than I did, anyway."

"If you're going to continue to beat yourself up about this," she said, "you're not going to do Rick much good, and you're going to get pretty annoying."

He looked at her and then smiled.

"You speak your mind, don't you?"

"Every chance I get."

"Well, I wouldn't want to annoy you," he said, "so I'll do my self-beating in private."

"Thank you. Come this way."

She led Clint through the corridors of the hospital, and stopped outside a room.

"Why is there no policeman outside his room?" he asked.

"You'll have to take that up with the police," she said.

"Meanwhile, Rick won't have anybody in the room with him. He can't see them, and he doesn't trust anyone he can't see."

"Can't see them?" Clint asked. "Why not?"

"You'll see," she said. "Brace yourself, it's not a pretty sight."

She opened the door and they both went in.

"Who is it? Who's there?" Rick demanded immediately.

"It's me, Rick. It's Grace, and I brought a friend."

Clint stared at Rick, who was lying on his stomach, his back swathed in bandages. The rage he felt was immeasurable.

"You didn't tell me he'd been shot in the back," he whispered to Grace.

"I didn't know it mattered."

"Oh, it matters," he said. "A lot."

Ever since Clint had lost his closest friend, Jim Hickok, to a backshooter, he couldn't tolerate anyone who would do such a thing. He hated nothing like he hated a cowardly backshooter.

"Who is it?" Rick asked. "Who'd you bring? I told you, I don't trust anybody—"

"I hope you'll trust me, buddy," Clint said, moving up alongside the bed.

"Clint? Is that you? Goddamn! It's good to hear your voice."

"I would have been here sooner," Clint started to explain, but Rick didn't let him finish.

"It doesn't matter," he said. "I know you got here as soon as you could. Come up farther, where I can see you."

Clint moved to the top of the bed, and Rick turned his head to look at him.

"Damn doctor says I can't lie on my back. You ever try lying on your belly all day?"

"Once."

"That's right," Rick said. "You were backshot yourself, once. So you know it's no fun."

"No fun at all," Clint said.

"Did Grace tell you what happened?"

"Only that you were shot," Clint said. "She left out the part about you being shot in the back."

"Give her a break," Rick said. "She doesn't know how much you hate that. She's a good woman, Clint. If it wasn't for her I'd probably be dead. She got me over here pretty quick."

"I'll have to thank her properly."

"You stay away from her, my friend," Rick said. "I won't be flat on my belly forever, and when I get back on my feet that little lady and I are going to finish what we started."

"You got it, old friend," Clint said. "Hands off."

"Does the 'good woman' have anything to say about it?" Grace asked.

"No," both men answered.

She came to stand next to Clint so Rick could see her. Clint thought his friend looked pale and thin.

"Tell me what happened," Clint said. "Who shot you?"

"I wish I knew," Rick said. "All I know is I was coming back from doing some gambling in Portsmouth Square at the Alhambra when it felt like somebody stuck a hot poker in my back. I only became aware of the shot after I was falling. Isn't that odd?"

"Any possibility somebody followed you from the square, wanted your winnings?"

"What makes you think I won?"

"You're a gambler who always manages to win."

"Well, you're right. I did win, but the shooter made no attempt to get to my money. I'm not even sure if he was standing behind me with a gun, or up on a roof with a rifle."

"Why is there no policeman outside your door standing guard?" Clint asked.

"That might have something to do with the fact I managed to alienate myself from the local law by taking a lot of money off of a certain police lieutenant at a poker table."

"That's no excuse."

"They think it was a robbery gone bad," Rick said. "They don't see any reason why the man would come back and try to rob me again, in a hospital."

"Did you tell them your suspicions about the other potential buyers?"

"I think Lieutenant Rawlins's exact words were, 'Each of them buyers is a gentleman and a businessman. Why would any of them want to shoot you?' "

"Like gentlemen and businessmen don't shoot people?" Clint asked. "What corner has this lieutenant been spending his life in?" He turned to Grace. "Do you know this fella?"

"I know Lieutenant Rawlins only too well," she said. "I'll be happy to introduce him to you. I'd like to see his face when he finds out who you are. The same goes for those other three businessmen." She said "businessmen" like it was a dirty word.

"All right," Clint said. He turned his head to say something to Rick, but noticed his friend was nodding off. "We'll get going and let you rest."

"Damn stuff they're giving me for the pain," Rick said.

Clint leaned down so Rick could see him and hear him clearly.

"I'm gonna catch this sonofabitch, Rick. You can count on it."

"I am counting on it."

"And I'm going to find somebody to stay in this room with you and keep you safe."

"I'll trust anybody you come up with, Clint."

Clint turned to Grace. "What's happening with your negotiations for the hotel?"

"I put them on hold when Rick was shot."

"How did the others feel about that?"

"They're all angry, but that too bad."

"Why not just sell to Rick?"

Before Grace could answer Rick said, "Don't put her on the spot like that, Clint. This is a business proposition and Grace has to make the best deal for herself. I don't expect her to sell me the hotel just because I got shot. One's got nothing to do with the other."

"Doesn't sound that way to me," Clint said. Before Grace could comment, he added, "Let's get out of here. We can talk back at your hotel, after I get settled."

"I'll pay for his room, Grace," Rick said.

"Nonsense," Grace said, "nobody's paying for his room. I think Clint is going to be working to help both of us, Rick."

"I am?"

She faced him, her eyes fiery.

"I want to know who shot Rick because that's a man I would never sell my hotel to. As long as you're trying to find that man, you won't have to spend a dime in my hotel."

"That sounds like a good deal to me," Rick said.

"Shut up and go to sleep," Clint said. "We'll see you in the morning."

Before they got to the door Clint could hear Rick snoring. He stopped Grace in the hall.

"Could you have someone put my gear in my room, and take my horse to a nearby livery stable? And be careful, because he's ornery. He was out to pasture and I had to press him back into service for this."

"Okay," she said, "but aren't you coming back to the hotel?"

"Not tonight," he said. "I didn't want Rick to know,

but I'll be spending the night out here in a chair."

"But . . . you can't. You're exhausted from traveling. Do you really think the man who shot him will try to get him in here?"

"First of all," Clint said, "I think we're dealing with more than one man. These businessmen would not dirty their own hands. So I'm going to want the man who pulled the trigger, and the man who paid him."

"I see," she said. "That makes sense."

"And second, Rick makes a much easier target lying in here on his stomach than he made out on the street."

"Another good point."

"So I'll rest as best I can in a chair with my back leaning against his door."

"You must be hungry," she said. "I'll bring you something to eat and drink."

"I'd appreciate that, Grace."

She stared at him for a moment, making him uncomfortable.

"What is it?"

"I don't think I've ever known a man to have a better friend than you, Clint," she said. "I admire you for your loyalty to Rick."

"He'd do the same thing for me."

"Are you sure?"

"I am," he said, "but even if he wouldn't, it doesn't matter. This is the only way I know how to be a friend."

"Well," she said, "it seems like a damned good way, to me."

THIRTEEN

True to her word, Grace brought Clint something to eat and drink that evening—and, in fact, sat out in the hall and ate and drank beer with him.

"Do you know anyone in San Francisco you can trust?" she asked him.

"I did, at one time, but it seems most of the people I know, or trust, don't live to a very ripe old age. There are men I could send for, but it would take them a while to get here."

"What will you do, then?"

"With your help I'd like to send a telegram to a friend of mine in Denver."

"Denver? Can he get here quickly?"

"I'll only be asking him to recommend someone here who can be trusted, not to come here himself."

"Is he friendly with Rick?"

"Not particularly," Clint said. "I'm friends with both of them, but they aren't friends with each other."

"I have friends like that, as well. What does this friend of yours do?" she asked.

"He's the best private detective in the business."

"I thought that was supposed to be Allan Pinkerton."

"Allan Pinkerton thinks that, too. My friend's name is
Talbot Roper, and he once worked for Pinkerton."

"And he'll know someone here who is trustworthy?"

"He knows somebody everywhere," Clint said. "He'll
have someone here at the hospital the day after I contact
him."

"Well, then write up your telegram and I'll send it on
my way back here in the morning."

"You don't have to come back, early," he said. "You
need your rest, too."

"I'll be back here to have breakfast with you," she said.

"And what are you going to do about your other potential buyers?" he asked.

"They'll have to wait until Rick is well enough to continue," she said.

"What if they don't want to wait?"

"Then they can leave," she said. "To tell you the truth
I can't negotiate with any of them until I know which one
of them had Rick shot. You said it earlier today and I
pooh-poohed it, but that man really is trying to steal my
hotel."

Seeing the look in Grace Morgan's eyes, Clint decided
that he was glad he wasn't that man.

Clint spent a fitful night in a chair in front of Rick's room,
virtually sleeping with his hand on his gun. In the morning
when Grace reappeared with breakfast and hot coffee, she
had a man with her. He was tall and fit, dark hair graying
at the temples. He looked to be in his late forties.

"Clint Adams, this is Doctor Robert Bentley," Grace
said, making the introductions. "He saved Rick's life."

"I'm very grateful to you, Doctor," Clint said. "Rick's
a good friend of mine."

"If you're a close friend perhaps there's something I
should tell you," the doctor said.

"What's that?"

"Mr. Hartman is not quite out of the woods, yet."

"What do you mean? He's going to recover, isn't he?"

"He's going to live," Doctor Bentley said, "but he may never walk again."

"What?"

"Right now he's paralyzed from the waist down."

"And . . . he's not going to recover the use of his legs?"

"It's too soon to tell," Bentley said. "The bullet did a lot of damage, and there's quite a bit of swelling there. We really won't know anything for sure until that swelling goes down."

"So how long will it be before we know?"

"Seven to ten days should tell us something."

Clint sank back down into the chair he had spent the night in.

"Have you told him this?"

"No, no," Bentley said, "there's no need to bother him with this now. We don't want to adversely affect his will to recover. And if he regains movement in his lower extremities, there won't any reason to ever tell him."

"I understand," Clint said, "and I completely agree."

"And I have another diagnosis."

"What's that?"

"If you don't get some rest you're not going to be any good to anyone," the physician said. "You look like hell."

"He traveled a long way to get here," Grace explained, "and hasn't been to sleep, yet."

"You spent the night out here?"

"Someone has to watch over Rick, Doc," Clint said. "Somebody tried to kill him."

"Well, shouldn't that be the job of the police?"

"You would think so," Clint said. "I should have somebody in the room with him by the end of the day."

"Well, you can't remain here until then," he said.

"I can manage."

"I think I can exert some influence and get a policeman

posted outside the door," Bentley said. "That would enable you to get some rest, and work on having someone sit with him while he recovers."

"If you could do that then I'd be doubly grateful, Doctor."

Bentley smiled and said, "I'll see what I can do." He turned to the fiery redhead and said, "Grace," kissing her before going off down the hall.

"And what's going on there?" he asked.

"Nothing," she said, then added, "anymore."

"And who ended it, you or him?"

"His wife. You want to eat this before it gets cold?"

By noon Dr. Bentley returned with a young uniformed policeman in tow.

"Clint Adams, this young man is Officer Jed Bentley."

"Bentley?"

"Yes," the doctor said, "he's my son."

"So then you're not here officially?"

"I have the day off, sir," Jed said. "I'm doing this as a favor for my father."

Jed Bentley looked like he didn't even shave yet, yet there was some steely resolve in his eyes.

"You'll be doing me a favor, too, then," Clint said. "One I won't forget."

"Don't mention it, sir."

Grace had told Clint that Bentley's word was good, and that he'd be able to trust whoever the good doctor put on the door. He wondered if she knew about Bentley's policeman son.

"You might as well go and get some sleep, Mr. Adams," Bentley said. "Jed and I can look after Mr. Hartman for a while."

"Thank you, again, Doctor," Clint said. "When I have the man I want I'll bring him in to introduce you to him."

"I could take some more time off, sir, and sit in the

room with Mr. Hartman," Jed Bentley said. "In plain clothes, of course."

"I'll keep that offer in mind, Officer Bentley," Clint said.

"Just call me Jed."

"Okay, Jed," Clint said. "I'll let you know if I need to take you up on the offer."

"Yes, sir," Jed said. "Any time."

"I'll walk you out," Doctor Bentley said.

As they reached the front door Bentley said, "Jed's very impressed by your reputation, Mr. Adams."

"And I take it you're not?"

"Oh, I'm impressed," the man said, "I just know how exaggerated some reputations can get."

"I certainly agree with that, Doctor," Clint said. "I'll see you later in the day—and thanks again for your help."

Clint left the hospital and headed for the Red Queen Hotel and a soft bed.

FOURTEEN

The beds at the Red Queen Hotel were the finest quality, and yet Clint still awoke after only four hours of sleep. He bathed and dressed and came down to the lobby. The man behind the front desk was not the same man—Benjamin—who had given him his key that morning when he arrived from the hospital. But apparently all of the front desk clerks had been alerted to his presence, and had been given his description.

"Good afternoon, Mr. Adams," the clerk said.

" 'Afternoon," Clint greeted him. He was older than Benjamin by several years. "What's your name?"

"Gordon, sir."

"Gordon, is the dining room open all day?"

"Yes, sir. They'll prepare you anything you want, sir, on the house. Those are Miss Morgan's instructions."

"They're good instructions," Clint said. "Thank you, Gordon."

"Yes, sir."

Clint started for the dining room, then stopped and came back to the desk.

"Gordon?"

"Sir?"

59

"Do you know all of the potential buyers Miss Morgan is negotiating with?"

"Yes, sir."

"Are any of them in the dining room right now?"

"I believe Mr. Castle is, sir."

"Castle?"

"Yes, sir."

"Jake Castle?"

"Yes, sir."

"Where is Miss Morgan?"

"I believe she's in her office. Shall I get her for you?"

"Why don't I just go back there and talk to her?"

"All right, sir," Gordon said. "Why don't you come around the desk and go on back."

"Thank you, Gordon."

"Sir."

Clint walked down the hall to Grace's office, thinking that Gordon the desk clerk was too good, and too damn polite, to be true.

When he reached the door he knocked.

"Come in."

He entered.

"Clint." She stood up from behind her desk immediately. "How are you feeling? I thought you'd sleep longer."

"So did I."

"Was the bed okay?"

"The bed was great."

She frowned. "What's wrong?"

"I just found out that one of your potential buyers is Jake Castle."

"Jake—you mean John Castle?"

"John Castle's 'friends' call him 'Jake.' "

"You know Mr. Castle?"

"I do," Clint said. "Out here we call him a gambler.

Back east, where he comes from, they call him a gangster."

"Gangster?"

"Criminal," Clint said. "Crime boss. Mr. Castle comes from New York."

"That much I knew," she said, "but I didn't know any of these other things you've mentioned. Do you think this man had Rick shot?"

"It's certainly the way he does business," Clint said, "but that doesn't mean he did it. It was just interesting to find out he was one of the buyers." He seated himself across from her as she sat back down. "Who are the other buyers?"

"One is a man named Wayne Jackson, and the other is Edward O'Brien. Do you know either of them?"

"No, I don't," Clint said. "Could be they're just legitimate businessmen."

"Well, I know that Mr. O'Brien owns quite a few hotel properties in the west. Mr. Jackson, I believe, comes here from somewhere near Chicago."

"Well, I'm about to go into the dining room to sample your food, and according to your man, Gordon, Jake Castle is in there, already."

"Are you saying there may be a confrontation?"

"I'm saying I'm going to go in there and confront him," Clint said. "Jake and I don't like each other. There's no way we can be in the same room and ignore each other."

"Will there be . . . violence?"

"No," Clint said, "not if I can help it." He stood up and walked to the door, then stopped and added, "unless he admits he had Rick shot. Then I'll probably kill him."

Clint returned to the lobby and entered the dining room, trying to look for Jake Castle without seeming to. He spotted him seated in a corner, eating alone. Briefly, he considered getting his own table, but then decided he might as well take the most direct route.

"Mr. Adams, I presume?" Clint was impressed that the dining room had a maitre d', even in the afternoon. "Can I get you a table, sir?"

"No, that's okay," Clint said, "I'm joining a . . . friend."

FIFTEEN

Jake Castle spotted Clint as he was crossing the room to his table. He put his knife and fork down on the table, but continued to chew his food lazily, almost like a grazing cow. Clint knew that Castle carried a gun in a shoulder harness under his left arm, and he knew the man knew how to use it.

"Hello, Adams," Castle said, around a piece of steak that was apparently stuck in his teeth. "Have a seat. The food here is excellent."

"That's what I've heard, Jake."

Clint sat down opposite Castle, and a waiter magically appeared at his elbow.

"I'll have what Mr. Castle is having."

"Yes, sir, steak and potatoes."

"Throw some eggs on there, too," Clint said, "and a pot of coffee."

"Yes, sir."

"Late breakfast?" Castle asked, picking up his utensils again.

"I had a late night," Clint said. "A friend of mine is in the hospital and I spent the night making sure nobody killed him."

Castle squinted across the table at Clint. He was built like a bull, with almost no neck, and while he had the appearance of a New York street thug Clint knew there was intelligence behind the brutish appearance. He was, as usual, wearing a very expensive black suit.

"You talkin' about Hartman?"

"That's right."

Castle put his knife and fork down again, sat back, and started to shake with silent laughter.

"What's so funny, Jake?"

Castle shook his head and said, "Oh, I'm not laughing at you, Adams. I'm just feeling sorry for whoever had Hartman shot, now that they've got you on their trail."

"So that would mean it wasn't you . . . right?"

"Me?" Abruptly, Castle stopped laughing. "Why would I have Rick Hartman shot?"

"I understand he was your main competition to buy this hotel and casino."

Castle sat forward and reclaimed his utensils. He started cutting into his meat.

"If I killed everyone who outbid me for a hotel I'd probably deserve the overblown reputation I have in New York."

"As a killer, you mean?"

Castle stuffed a huge piece of steak into his mouth and said, "That's the one."

"Well, I never thought I'd say this," Clint replied, "but we agree, Jake."

"If I had done it, Adams, he would have been shot head on," Castle said. "That's how I do business, face to face. And I'll tell you another thing, I would have done it myself. Those other two—if they did it, mind you—wouldn't have pulled the trigger themselves, they'd have hired it done."

"Thanks for the insight, Jake," Clint said. "I'll keep that in mind."

"I think you're looking for a hired gunman," Castle went on.

"In that case I'll want both," Clint said. "The man who pulled the trigger, and the man who paid him."

"That's one of the things I like about you, Adams," Castle said. "You're thorough. Listen, I'm done here, you don't mind if I leave while you're still eating, so you?"

"Go ahead," Clint said. "It's not like I'm your guest."

Castle stood and left some money on the table and said, "That should cover it. Listen, I hope you catch the bastard, I really do. In fact, if I can help, let me know."

"I'll do that, Jake."

"You and me ain't always seen eye to eye in the past," Castle said, "but I respect you, and I think you respect me."

"I guess that's true."

"So with respect," Castle said, "I had nothing to do with your friend being shot."

Castle left without waiting for Clint to say whether he believed him or not.

SIXTEEN

As Clint came back from the dining room through the lobby the desk clerk, Gordon, called him over.

"There's a man waiting for you, Mr. Adams."

"What man?"

"He wouldn't give me his name," Gordon said, shaking his head. "He claims he's here in response to some telegram."

"Where is he?" Clint asked. Talbot Roper had come through, sending a man in reply instead of a telegram of his own.

"He's sitting right over there," the clerk said, inclining his head.

Clint turned and saw a man seated on one of the lobby sofas.

"Oh, by the way," Gordon added, "you also got a telegram."

Clint accepted it, saw that it was from Roper. His friend had obviously sent two replies.

"Thanks, Gordon."

"Yes, sir."

Clint decided to read the telegram before meeting the man. He tore it open right there at the desk.

CLINT

    BY THE TIME YOU READ THIS THERE SHOULD BE
A MAN WAITING IN THE LOBBY TO SEE YOU. HIS
NAME'S JOE RENO. YOU CAN TRUST HIM ALMOST AS
MUCH AS YOU CAN TRUST ME. GOOD LUCK.

                              TAL ROPER

P.S. DON'T LET HIS APPEARANCE FOOL YOU.

    Clint folded the telegram up and slipped it into his
pocket before walking across the lobby.
    "Are you waiting to see me?" he asked the man on the
sofa.
    "Joe Reno," the man said, standing. He hardly came up
to Clint's shoulder, but when the two men shook hands
Clint noticed that his grip was that of a man three times
his size. He was young, maybe thirty or so, and was wearing a suit that was not expensive, but fit him perfectly.
Clint could see the bulge his gun made beneath his arm.
    "I got a telegram from Mr. Roper in Denver, said you
needed some help."
    "That's true," Clint said. "Have you eaten anything to-
day?"
    "Not really."
    "Well, come on, I'll buy you some lunch and we can talk."
    "All right, sir."
    Clint found himself going into the dining room for the
second time that afternoon.

Clint bought Reno a steak meal and had another pot of
coffee for himself. He explained the situation with Hartman, how the shooting happened and what his condition
was now.
    "So how long will he be in the hospital?"
    "I don't know," Clint said, "but I'll want you there for
as long as it takes."

Reno shrugged and said, "I'm yours."

"Let's talk about your fee."

"No fee."

"What? Why not?"

"Tal Roper asked me to do this. That's reason enough for me."

"Maybe so, but you've still got to make a living."

"Mr. Adams, how about you just pay my expenses . . . and keep feeding me like this."

"You've got a deal," Clint said, shaking Reno's hand.

"Just one thing."

"What's that?"

"I'll need to bring in another man to spell me. I'm not gonna do anybody any good if I can't keep my eyes open."

"Okay," Clint said, "but Roper told me I can trust you as I'd trust him. Will that be true of this other man?"

"I don't know if you can trust him the way you would Roper," Reno said, "but you'll be able to trust him as much as you do me."

"Okay," Clint said.

"One thing, though," Reno said. "You'll have to pay his fee."

"No problem." Clint stood up. "I'm going to leave you to finish your meal. Meet me in the lobby in half an hour. Do you need to buy any special gear?"

"I've got all my own stuff, sir," Reno said.

"You're going to have to stop calling me 'sir,' " Clint said, "and start calling me Clint."

"Okay, Clint."

"I'll see you later."

This time when Clint reentered the lobby the desk clerk didn't bother him. He noticed, however, that Gordon had given way to Benjamin. He walked over to the desk.

"Benjamin."

"Good afternoon, Mr. Adams."

"Do you know where Mr. Jackson or Mr. O'Brien are?"

"I believe Gordon told me he saw Mr. Jackson going into the casino," the young man answered. "I don't know where Mr. O'Brien is."

"Describe Jackson to me."

"Tall, about forty-five, black hair that comes to a point right in the center of his forehead. Real distinctive lookin', I think."

"And Mr. O'Brien?"

"Older, fatter, looks like a banker."

"Okay, thanks."

Clint decided he had time to make the acquaintance of Wayne Jackson before meeting up with Reno again in the lobby. He headed for the casino.

SEVENTEEN

When Clint entered the casino he was impressed. As with the hotel lobby, this rivaled some of the places in Portsmouth Square, just on a smaller scale. What it lacked in size it more than made up for in quality.

There were five steps down to get to the casino floor, but he remained on the top landing, looking the place over. He was looking for that distinctive widow's peak that Benjamin had described Wayne Jackson as having. When he spotted the man at a blackjack table he descended the steps and walked over.

You can tell a lot about a man by the way he gambles. Clint stood and watched a few hands and noticed that Jackson was reckless, splitting cards when he shouldn't have and doubling his bet without any apparent reason. He wondered if the man did business that way, or if this was his outlet for those tendencies.

There were empty chairs on either side of Jackson, as it was still early in the day. Clint sat on the man's right, because then there was no one seated on his own gun side.

He bought some chips from the dealer and played one or two hands before waiting for a lull when the dealer had to introduce a new deck.

"Mr. Jackson?"

The man looked at him and said, "That's right. Do I know you?"

"No, sir," Clint said, "I just wanted to introduce myself. My name's Clint Adams."

"Should that mean something to me?" Jackson asked, stacking and restacking his chips. Clint had the feeling it did, but the man did not want to show it.

"I'm a friend of Rick Hartman's."

"Ah," Jackson said, "the gunman."

"Then you have heard of me."

Jackson stacked his chips one last time and then looked at Clint.

"Well, I'd be a fool to claim I'd never heard of the Gunsmith," he said. "What is it I can do for you, Mr. Adams?"

"I'm going to find out who ordered Rick to be shot, Mr. Jackson," he said. "I'm going to find both men involved."

"Both?"

"The man who pulled the trigger and the man who paid him," Clint said. "I just wanted you to know that."

The dealer was ready to go, but Jackson held his hand up to stop him. He and Clint were the only players at the table, and they were not ready.

"Why are you telling me this, Mr. Adams?"

"I'm telling everyone, Mr. Jackson," Clint replied. "I've told Mr. Castle, and now you, and I'll be telling Mr. O'Brien, as soon as I find him."

"That should be rich," Jackson said.

"Why is that?"

"O'Brien's a banker," the man said. "You're going to scare him to death."

"But I don't scare you?"

"No, Mr. Adams," Jackson said, "you don't scare me.

You see, I didn't have anything to do with Hartman being shot, so I have no reason to fear you."

"That's good, Mr. Jackson," Clint said, "if you're telling the truth. If you're not, however, I'll find out, and then you'd have reason to fear me because I'll give you one."

Clint had bought fifty dollars worth of chips and had made it into a hundred in two hands. Now he pushed all his chips forward and said to the dealer, "Deal."

Jackson did not play, but watched as the dealer gave Clint an Ace of Spades, and a King of Spades for blackjack. That gave Clint two hundred and fifty dollars in chips.

"These are for you," he said to the dealer, pushing the chips toward the man.

"Thank you, sir!" the dealer said.

Clint looked at Wayne Jackson and said, "Remember what I just told you—and stop splitting your cards so often."

EIGHTEEN

Clint met up with Joe Reno in the lobby and took him over to the hospital to introduce him to Rick Hartman. When they reached the door to Rick's room, Joe Reno and Officer Bentley stood nose to nose.

"What's he doing here, Mr. Adams?" Bentley asked.

"Reno's working for me, Jed," Clint said. "He'll be staying in Rick's room. We won't need you to sit out here anymore."

"Yes, sir," Bentley said. "That's your decision to make."

Clint took Reno into the room.

"Pleased to meet you, Joe," Hartman said. "Can't tell you what a relief it will be to have somebody watching my back—so I don't get shot again!"

"It's not gonna happen on my watch, Mr. Hartman," Reno said. "That I guarantee."

"Are you a private detective here in town?" Rick asked.

"Oh, no sir," Reno said. "I'm not a private detective like Mr. Roper. I'm just a fella who does odd jobs."

"Rick, Joe is going to bring in a second man we can trust," Clint explained.

"He should be here tonight to relieve me," Reno said.

75

"You've already arranged that?" Clint asked.

Reno smiled a bit sheepishly and said, "I knew I was going to take this job."

The smile made Clint revise his guess of the man's age. He'd thought him to be thirty or so, but the smile took several years off of that estimate. Talbot Roper must have been pretty high on this young man to recommend him.

"What's the other man's name?" Clint asked.

"Stryker," Reno said, "Andy Stryker."

"A private detective, or an odd job man, like you?" Clint asked.

"Stryker sort of does what he wants," Reno said. "We're friends, so he agreed to help. His rates are high, but I didn't think that would be a problem since you're only covering my expenses."

"Money's not a problem."

"Well, he's worth his rates," Reno said. "Good man with a knife and a gun, and he's deadly in hand-to-hand combat."

"We'll take your recommendation, Joe," Rick said.

"Thank you, sir."

"And you'll have to call me Rick."

"Yes, sir, I'll do that."

"I spoke with Wayne Jackson today," Clint said to Rick, "and Jake Castle. Why didn't you tell me about Castle?"

"Damn painkillers," Rick said, his words muffled by his pillow. "I didn't think of it last night. You and Jake go at it today?"

"We had lunch together," Clint said.

"You had lunch with Jake Castle?" Reno asked.

"You know of him?" Clint asked.

"Sure," Reno said, but didn't elaborate on how or from where.

"Well, Jake says he didn't shoot you or have anybody

else do it," Clint said to Rick, "and Wayne Jackson pretty much said the same thing."

"What else would they say?" Rick asked. "Who'd you believe?"

"I sort of believed Jake," Clint said. "He was telling the truth when he said that if he shot you, you'd have seen him coming."

"Probably."

Clint looked at Reno.

"You having a change of heart now that you know Castle is involved?"

"No, sir."

"What about your friend, Stryker? Will he have a change of heart?"

"Andy's not afraid of anyone, Mr. Adams," Reno said. "Sometimes I think that's his only fault."

"What's your next move?" Rick asked.

"O'Brien," Clint said. "Jackson said he's a banker who'd probably be scared to death of me."

"I doubt it," Rick said. "O'Brien may be a banker, but he's pretty steady. I think there's more of a chance that Jackson would be scared of you."

"Well, he put up a pretty good front."

"He seems the type."

"I'm going to leave Joe here with you, Rick," Clint said. "I'll come back tonight so I can meet Andy Stryker."

"Okay, Clint," Rick said, "just remember to watch your own back while you're doing this."

"That's not something I'd forget to do," Clint said.

When he left the room he found Jed Bentley still waiting there in the hall.

"Mr. Adams, I don't know if you realize who Joe Reno is."

"Walk out with me, Jed."

The two men started through the halls. Bentley was still in his uniform.

"Reno came highly recommended to me, Jed."

"He's a criminal."

"That may be," Clint said, "but that's not my concern, right now. My only concern is my friend's safety, and I've been assured that Reno and his friend can protect him."

"His friend?"

"Yes," Clint said, "a man named Stryker."

"Andy Stryker?"

"That's right."

"Sir, he's a bigger criminal than Reno is!"

They reached the front door and stopped there.

"Jed, all I care about is that the men I'm using to protect Rick are capable," Clint explained. "If you tell me these two men aren't, then I'll look elsewhere."

"It's not that," Jed said. "They're very capable men—they're just not honest men."

"Well, honesty is the least of my worries now," Clint said. "If the police had done their job—well, I don't want to get into that."

"You're talking about Lieutenant Rawlins."

"What do you know about him?"

"He's not my boss," Jed said. "He's a superior officer, but he's a detective, so I don't work under him."

"Are you avoiding my question?" Clint asked. "You're concerned with honesty, so what do you know about him?"

"All right," Jed said, "so he's not very honest or trustworthy . . ."

"See? There are men like that on both sides of the law," Clint said. "Right now I'm concerned with physical abilities, not moral strength."

"I understand," Jed said. "If there's anything else I can

do to help, let me know. You can get in touch through my father."

"Thanks for your help, Jed," Clint said. "I'll be in touch."

"Yes, sir."

Clint let Jed go down the stairs first and watched him walk off, an honest young man who was in for a rude awakening as he got older and older.

NINETEEN

When Clint returned to the Red Queen there was another man waiting for him in the lobby. This man was not in uniform, but had an official bearing to him. He was in his late forties and sported an impressive mustache which seemed to completely mask his mouth. Even before Clint met him, he felt he knew who he was.

"Mr. Adams?" the man asked, approaching.

"That's right."

"My name is Rawlins," he said, "Lieutenant Rawlins. I'm with the San Francisco Police Department."

"Have I broken some law already?" Clint asked. "I only just arrived in town last night."

"No," Rawlins said, "no law that I know of. I just thought it would be a good idea if we talked."

"About what?"

"About why you came to San Francisco."

"That's easy," Clint said. "I like to gamble."

"I see. That's the only reason?"

"Well, no," Clint said, "now that you mention it. My friend was shot down in the street and the police department here doesn't seem to want to do anything about it."

"And you will?"

"Oh yes," Clint said, "I will. I'll find the man or men responsible."

The lieutenant looked around and saw that they were the center of attention for the few people who were in the lobby.

"Perhaps we can go somewhere else and talk about this?" he suggested.

"Well, unless you want to take me to the police station," Clint said, "this suits me just fine."

Rawlins looked annoyed, but did not make a scene.

"Very well. I assume you're talking about Rick Hartman being shot?" the policeman asked.

"That's who I'm talking about, yes," Clint said.

"What makes you think the police are doing nothing about it?"

"There was not a policeman assigned to protect him in the hospital," Clint said. "What if his assailant tried again?"

"The matter is under investigation, Mr. Adams," Lieutenant Rawlins said, "I assure you, but it's fairly obvious that your friend was the victim of a robbery attempt. Why would a robber want to try again in the hospital?"

"What makes you think it was a robbery attempt?"

"As I said," Rawlins repeated, "the matter is under investigation. Your friend was returning from a night of gambling in Portsmouth Square. Robbers very often follow people from there to steal their winnings from them."

"Nothing was stolen from Rick."

"Apparently the attempt went awry."

"And that's it?" Clint asked. "That's the extent of your investigation?"

"The case has not been closed," Rawlins said. "We are searching for the guilty party."

"Well, just so you know," Clint replied, "so am I."

"And what do you intend to do when you find them?"

"I don't know," Clint answered. "I guess I'll decide that when the time comes."

Rawlins took several steps closer to Clint and lowered his voice.

"I have to warn you that I'd take a dim view of you exacting some sort of revenge for your friend's death," Rawlins said. "San Francisco is not the wild west, Mr. Adams. Your usual tactics won't be tolerated here, where we are more civilized."

"And what do you think you know about my tactics, Lieutenant Rawlins?"

"Your reputation precedes you, I'm afraid."

"Well then," Clint said, "so does yours."

"I know all about you, Mr. Adams," Rawlins said, "and you know absolutely nothing about me."

"I wouldn't be too sure of that, Lieutenant."

Rawlins stepped past Clint, then turned to face him.

"I'll be watching you, Adams."

"Is that a threat?"

"It's a warning," Rawlins said, and left.

Clint turned to find Grace Morgan coming toward him. She was wearing a simple dress today, covered to the neck, with no sequins or baubles to enhance it. Obviously not a dress she did any of her evening casino business with.

"That didn't look very friendly," she said.

"According to the lieutenant," Clint said, "it was civilized."

"He didn't ask you to leave San Francisco, did he?"

"No, not yet," Clint said. "Just a warning that he'd be watching me."

"Did you get everything settled at the hospital?" she asked.

"Yes," Clint said, "Rick will be looked after, so now I'm free to start searching for the men responsible for shooting him."

"I understand you spoke with Mr. Castle and Mr. Jackson?"

"Yes, earlier today."

"Mr. O'Brien came to my office today."

"And?"

"He assumes you'll want to speak with him as well, so he's invited you to have dinner with him tonight in the dining room."

"Well," Clint said, "it will be nice not to have to go looking for him. You can tell him for me that I accept his invitation, with pleasure."

TWENTY

And so another meeting took place in the Red Queen's dining room, which Clint didn't mind. The food was excellent.

Edward O'Brien did, indeed, resemble the banker that he was. A portly, well-dressed gentleman, his hair was thinning so that his scalp gleamed through, and he wore wire-framed glasses which he removed when Clint approached his table.

"Mr. Adams?" He extended his hand. Standing, he was barely five-and-a-half feet tall.

"That's right."

"A pleasure to meet you, sir," O'Brien said. "I hope it wasn't presumptuous of me, but I ordered two glasses of red wine."

It was presumptuous, as Clint didn't like wine all that much, but he said, "That's fine."

"Good, good," O'Brien said, "please, have a seat."

Both men sat down and a waiter appeared with the two glasses of wine.

"Would you gentlemen care to order?"

O'Brien raised his eyebrows at Clint, who said, "Steak is fine with me."

O'Brien said, "I'll have the beef stew."

The waiter nodded and left to put in their orders.

"Thank you for agreeing to meet me for dinner," the banker said.

"Since I wanted to talk to you anyway," Clint said, "it seemed like a good idea."

O'Brien tasted his wine and set the glass back down. Clint left his where it sat.

"I understand from Miss Morgan that you are here to investigate the shooting of Mr. Hartman, who is a friend of yours."

"Rick is my friend," Clint said, "but I don't know if investigate is the right word. I'm not a detective. I do, however, plan to find the man who shot him—and the man who hired it done."

"You're quite certain there are two men?"

"At least."

"I see," O'Brien said. "There could have been more, of course. So I am . . . suspected of being one of them?"

"It's a possibility."

"Well, would it put your mind at ease if I told you I had nothing to do with it?"

Clint smiled. "Only if I believed you."

O'Brien looked stunned.

"I give you my word, sir."

"Mr. O'Brien," Clint said, "since we've only just met I have no idea what your word is worth."

"My word is my bond in my business."

"Well," Clint said, "we're not doing business, are we?"

"Well, as a matter of fact," O'Brien said, "that is something I wanted to discuss with you. I would like you to come to work for me."

Over their dinners, banker Edward O'Brien went into more detail about what he wanted Clint to do for him.

"I am actually offering to pay you to do what you're doing, anyway," the man said.

"And that is?"

"Find the man who shot Rick Hartman."

"And why would you want to pay me to do that?"

"Because the faster that matter is cleared up," he explained, "the faster Miss Morgan will make her decision about who she is going to sell this hotel to."

"I see."

"I believe I was the front-runner, you see," O'Brien said, "but the shooting has held things up."

"You don't think she was intending to sell to Castle or Jackson? Or Rick Hartman?"

"I think it was between me and Mr. Hartman." He stopped chewing and put his silverware down, looking stricken. For a moment Clint thought he was having a heart attack. "Oh dear, I believe I might have just given myself a motive."

Clint studied the man. Supposedly, he was a successful banker, so he couldn't possibly be as dumb as he was trying to lead Clint to believe. So maybe he was just that smart.

"Mr. O'Brien," Clint said, "Miss Morgan really hasn't told me who she was leaning toward selling to, and yes, you have just given yourself a good motive to want Rick Hartman out of the way."

"I would never kill a man—or have a man killed—to ensure a business deal, Mr. Adams."

"Maybe you didn't want him killed," Clint said. "Maybe you just wanted him out of the way, and you didn't realize that Miss Morgan would hold the matter up as a result of his injury."

O'Brien frowned.

"So I can't convince you of my innocence?"

"Not just yet," Clint said. "Not with a steak dinner and a glass of wine."

"And not with my offer of employment?"

"I won't take money to find the men responsible for shooting my friend, Mr. O'Brien," Clint said. "Finding them and making them pay will be a pleasure."

He smiled across the table at the banker and lifted the wineglass to his lips.

TWENTY-ONE

After dinner with the banker O'Brien, Clint decided to check out the casino in the evening. When he entered the first thing he saw was the red-haired Grace Morgan walking the floor in a jade green dress that was cut very low to show off her cleavage which, while not the deepest he'd ever seen, was still impressive. He remembered, though, that his friend was sweet on this woman, and lying helpless in the hospital. So, while his first instinct would normally have been to approach her and try to get her into bed, he quelled that and decided to concentrate on the gambling that was available.

Grace Morgan, however, may have had other ideas. When Clint came down the stairs she was strolling right over to him.

"Come to try your luck?" she asked.

He wasn't sure she meant with the games that were available, but he said, "Poker is my game, but I prefer a saloon game, or a private game to a casino-run game. I never like trying to buck the house."

"Sounds like you know what you're doing," she said. "If I come across a private game I'll let you know."

"Thanks."

"Meanwhile there are plenty of other games in town."

Maybe she wasn't as sweet on Rick as he was on her. Or maybe Clint's ego was just getting the better of him.

"I think I'll just walk around a bit," he said. He noticed there were three or four girls working the room. "You ladies look quite lovely."

"They're good," she said, "but maybe not in your league."

"Oh, I don't know," he said, "that dark-haired girl looks just my type."

The brunette was full-figured, reminded him a bit of the blonde he'd left in Labyrinth.

"If you like cows," she said. He thought it was an odd statement to make about one of her own girls.

"I usually like some meat on my women," he said.

"I see." She seemed to take that as an insult. "Well, I have work to do. Enjoy your evening."

She walked away and he breathed a sigh of relief. If she had pressed him he didn't know if he would have been able to resist her. She had one thing the other girls on the floor did not have, and that was maturity, which he found very attractive.

He looked up to see the brunette coming his way with an inviting smile on her face—and she did have very deep cleavage to entice him with.

Her name was Brandy and she took it upon herself to show him around. She linked her arm in his and as they walked side-by-side, she was just the right height for him to be able to fully enjoy and admire her breasts. Her cleavage was pale and full, with no space between her breasts and a very nice bounce that could easily become a juggle at a moment's notice. Of the girls on the floor—Brandy, a blonde named Delia, a somewhat-less-fiery-than-Grace redhead called Lucky, and a small Asian girl called Mai— Brandy seemed the oldest, though not yet thirty.

"Is blackjack your game?" she asked, stopping with him at one of the tables.

"On occasion," he said, "but if I had to concentrate on my cards I couldn't concentrate on you, could I?"

She smiled at the compliment and said, "I believe my employer would rather you concentrate on gambling than on me."

"I believe you're right," he said, although for totally different reasons than she thought.

They finally stopped at the roulette wheel and, since Clint didn't want Brandy to get fired for not doing her job, he decided to drop a few dollars chasing the number eight, which he simply picked at random. However, he played the number half a dozen times for ten dollars each time, and it came up half the time. He ended up with a profit of over a thousand dollars.

"My God!" Brandy said. "Are you always this lucky?"

"Not really," he said, tucking a hundred-dollar chip between her breasts. Rather than disappear as it might have on the other girls, it simply stuck there until she reached up and tucked it away out of sight.

"We better find something else for me to do," he said. "If I win too much your boss might get mad, fire you, and throw me out of the place."

"Don't worry," she said, patting his arm, "I'm sure we can find something you can lose at."

As they walked past a faro table a man bellowed, "There you are, gal," and reached out to grab her and pull her away from Clint. "Ever since you walked away I been losing my ass."

She squirmed to get out of his grasp, but he was holding her fast.

"I'm sorry," she said to him, "I can't stay with one person too long. I have to work the floor."

"You been walking around with this dude for a while," the man said, jerking his head at Clint.

Clint looked down at the black suit he was wearing and guessed he might have looked like a dude tonight. He didn't take offense at that, but he did take offense at the way the man was hanging onto Brandy.

TWENTY-TWO

Clint grabbed the man by the wrist and twisted until the man had two choices—let her go, or suffer a broken wrist.

"Ow!" the man cried out.

As he released Brandy she backed away from him, moving closer to Clint. The man stood up now and, flanked by two friends, faced Clint.

"What the hell you think you're doin'?" he demanded. "Ya coulda broke my wrist."

"You're right," Clint said. "I could have."

"Eddy," one of his friends said, "maybe you should just forget it."

"You gonna back my play or not?" Eddy hissed at his friend. "We back each other's play, don't we?"

"Yeah," the third man said, "but your plays always seem to be about women."

All three men were dressed more for Dodge City than San Francisco, and it was clear that the two men flanking Eddy didn't always like backing his play. They were all in their late twenties, although the two friends seemed to have a bit more sense than their friend.

"I think your friends are right, Eddy," Clint said. "Why

get into an argument over a woman who wants nothing to do with you?"

"Who says she don't?" Eddy demanded, sticking his jaw out.

"I do," Brandy said. "I don't want to have nothing to do with you, Mister."

Eddy looked at her and seemed about to cry.

"How about I buy you and your friends a drink and you go back to the table?" Clint offered. "Maybe your luck will change with a free drink."

"Yeah," one of the other men said, prodding Eddy, "how about a free drink?"

"Sounds like a good idea to me, Eddy," the third man said.

Eddy didn't look convinced, but he let his friends turn him and lead him back to his table.

"I'll get those drinks right over to you," Clint said. He turned to Brandy. "Are you all right?"

"I think so," she said, looking past him, "if I can hang on to my job."

He turned and saw that Grace Morgan had been watching them from across the room, and she seemed to be staring daggers at Brandy.

"I think you'll be okay," he said. "Can you arrange for these gentlemen's drinks?"

"Sure," she said, touching his arm, "and thanks."

Brandy went off to get their drinks and Clint walked across the floor to where Grace was standing.

"You diffused that pretty well," she said. "I thought there was going to be trouble."

"Nobody wanted trouble there, Grace."

"What was it about?"

Apparently, she had seen the events from the beginning and didn't know that the potential argument was about Brandy.

"A difference of opinion," he said.

"Well, I've seen differences of opinion like that erupt into gunplay," she said. "You sure you wouldn't like a job here, keeping the peace?"

"I've got a job," he said.

"Yes, finding out who shot Rick," she said, "but you're not getting paid for that one."

"Seems like I'm in demand today," he observed. "You're the second person to offer me a job."

"Mr. O'Brien?"

He nodded.

"He wanted to pay me to find the men who shot Rick."

"Why would he do that when you were already working on it?"

"He seems to think the quicker we get that out of the way the quicker he gets to buy your hotel."

"He said that?"

Clint nodded.

"He seems to think he's the front-runner."

She just nodded.

"Is he?" Clint asked.

"I'm not sure who the front-runner is, Clint," she said. "I do know one thing, though."

"What's that?"

"It's fun for a woman to keep these businessmen hanging."

She walked off and he watched her as she crossed the large room and found Brandy, carrying drinks to the three men at the faro table. She stopped the younger woman briefly, whispered in her ear, and then continued on, working the crowd. When Clint couldn't see her anymore he went and found Brandy, who was now on her way back from the faro table, having served the three men their free drinks.

"What did Grace say to you?" he asked.

Looking annoyed, she said, "She told me you were her

guest, and that I had better pay more attention to the paying customers."

"Did she threaten your job?"

"No," she said, "but it was implied."

"I'm sorry about that."

"We all knew she was sleeping with Mr. Hartman," Brandy observed. "Is she after you, now? Does she want to keep all the good-looking, interesting men for herself?"

"Maybe that's what it means to her to be the boss."

"Then why is she planning to sell?" Brandy asked. "None of us can figure that out."

"Maybe I should give it a try," he said.

TWENTY-THREE

Clint threw around some of the money he'd won at the roulette wheel and still went to his room with five hundred dollars profit. Grace Morgan had vanished for the rest of the night, so he never got a chance to talk to her again.

He had, however, spoken to all of the potential buyers, and had not come away with a feeling that one or the other was guilty. He thought they were all capable of having Rick Hartman shot to get him out of the way so they could buy the Red Queen, but had not yet formed an opinion.

When the knock came at his door he had removed his shirt and boots and was preparing to take off his pants and wash before going to bed. He took his gun from the holster hanging on the bedpost and moved to the door.

"Who is it?"

"It's Brandy," a girl's voice said, "from the casino?"

He opened the door with the gun held low and saw her standing in the hall alone. He stuck his head out to look back and forth, then relaxed when he was sure she was alone.

"What can I do for you, Brandy?" he asked.

"I asked the desk clerk what room you were in," she said. "I hope you don't mind."

"No, I don't mind."

"Can I come in?"

He hesitated, then said, "Sure," and backed up to allow her to enter. She came in and saw the gun.

"You can't be too careful," he said, closing the door. He walked to the bedpost and holstered the gun.

She stood in the center of the room, not nervous, but not comfortable. She was wearing a shawl over the low-cut dress she'd worn while working.

"I know about your friend being shot," she said. "And you're looking for the man who did it."

"That's right."

"I came up to warn you, Mr. Adams."

"Clint," he said, "just call me Clint. Warn me about what?"

She hesitated a moment, then said, "Those three men at the faro table? After you left they talked about getting even with you."

"For what?" he asked.

"For what you did for me."

"Sounded to me like that fella's two friends had more sense than him."

"They did," she said. "They said it would be better to ambush you than face you, on account of who you were."

Clint frowned.

"How'd they know who I was?"

"One of them said he recognized you," she answered. "That's why they stopped him when they did."

"And do you know who I am?"

"I do now," she said. "I mean, I recognized your name when they said it."

"Anybody else in the casino hear them talking?"

"The faro dealer."

"What's his name?"

"Tate."

"That's all?"

She shrugged.

"First or last name?"

She shrugged again.

"How long have you worked here, Brandy?"

"Just a few weeks."

That might explain why she didn't know everybody else's names yet, like some of the dealers.

"Do you know the names of the three men at the faro table?"

"I heard what you heard," she said. "Eddy."

"Okay," he said. "Is there anything else you know?"

"Well," she said, "one other thing."

"What's that?"

She dropped her shawl to the floor with a smile. "I know I don't want to go home tonight."

TWENTY-FOUR

In the morning Clint rolled over and bumped into a warm, delightfully fleshy hip. He had not had very much to drink last night, so the events that took place during the night were wonderfully clear. . . .

Brandy's dress soon followed her shawl to the floor and she stood in the middle of Clint's room, naked. Her body was full, her curves lush. She was a delightful reminder of the woman he had been with in Labyrinth recently. While he enjoyed women in all their shapes and forms, he was, of late, particularly enjoying fleshy women—and Brandy qualified. It seems he was faced with acres of pale, soft, smooth flesh, and he knew just what to do with it.

He approached her and she came eagerly into his arms. Locked in a hot embrace they fell to the bed together, their mouths fused together, tongues lashing. Together they managed to get his pants off and then she was kissing him, stroking him, bringing him to an amazing readiness. He grabbed her and flipped her over so she was on her back, and then explored her body with his tongue, spending a lot of time on her chubby breasts and turgid nipples, then kissing his way down her body, over her soft belly

until his tongue was delving into her pubic thatch, finding
her wet and ready. . . .

The night continued like that, each taking a turn pleasuring the other, until they both tumbled into an exhausted,
dreamless sleep. Now, with her warm hip pressed against
his, he felt himself getting hard again, wanting her again.
He turned so that he was spooning her, his erection
pressed into the cleft between her buttocks. She woke up,
felt him there, and wiggled her butt against him.

"Are you ready again?" she asked.

"It's morning," he said. "A brand new day."

He poked between her thighs with his penis and she
spread them so that he slid up and into her. She gasped
as he began to move in and out of her. They moved together, not losing contact, so that she was on her knees.
He took hold of her hips with both hands and she started
slapping her butt back against him so that the room filled
with the sound of flesh on flesh, both of them grunting
with the effort. Clint reached around in front of her to
pinch her nipples, paw her breasts, slide his hand down
over her belly and then to her wetness. As he fucked her
from behind he stroked her in front and before long her
body began to tremble with her need to explode . . . and
then she did . . . followed closely by him. . . .

Later she was lying on her back, her marvelous breasts
flattened out against her chest, still trying to catch her
breath.

"You sure can get a girl worked up in the morning,
Clint," she said, stretching.

He was getting dressed but paused to admire her while
she stretched.

"What are you looking at?" she demanded, playfully.

"You," he said, "your body."

She folded her hands across her breasts.

"Most of the men look at the other girls," she said, "the skinny ones. I wish I was skinny."

"No, no," he said, "that would be a crime. You should stay just the way you are. They may look at the other women, but you're the one they want to go to bed with."

"Well, I don't want to go to bed with them," she said. "Most of them are either pigs or losers . . . and some of them are both."

"You don't like losers?"

"I don't mean at the tables," she said, "I mean in life."

"Oh, I see."

"Like those three at the faro table. You will be careful with them, won't you?"

"I'm always careful, Brandy," he said. "That's how I've managed to live to a ripe old age."

She giggled, which made her flesh jiggle, and said, "Not so old."

"Believe me," he said, strapping on his gun belt, "for someone in my position, this is old."

TWENTY-FIVE

Clint went down for breakfast, his legs pleasantly shaky after a full night of Brandy. As he crossed the lobby he saw Joe Reno enter and wave at him.

"Had breakfast?" he asked.

"Not yet."

"Come on," Clint said. "I'll buy."

"Thanks."

They got situated at a table and ordered steak and eggs each.

"How'd it go last night?"

"Fine," Reno said. "I wanted to come in today and tell you that we'll just be doing two shifts."

"Just taking twelve hours each?"

Reno nodded.

"Figured the fewer men involved the less chance there'll be of anything going wrong."

"Sounds like a good plan."

"Stryker's over there now," Reno said. "He and your friend Rick started to get along right away."

"Rick gets along with people easily," Clint said, then added, "People he likes, that is."

"Stryker's the same way."

Their breakfast came and they broke off until the plates had been distributed and the waiter left.

"So how's your investigation going?" Reno asked.

"Don't know that I can call it an investigation," Clint said. "I talked to the other buyers involved, and I think they're all capable of having it done." The steak had been done perfectly.

"Do you need any help?"

"You've got enough to do, Joe," Clint said. "After twelve hours at the hospital you need to get some sleep."

"Four hours is all I need," Reno said. "That leaves me some extra time if you need anything else done."

"There is one thing you can help me with, since you'd obviously have more contacts here than I would."

"What's that?"

"I need to know if there are any professional gunmen in town," Clint said. "Men who hire out for this kind of work."

"You need to know if they are or have been in town," Joe Reno said.

"Right."

"I'll pass the word and see what I can find out. Considering the men you're dealing with here—men who can afford to buy a place like this—you probably want someone with a high asking price."

"Good point," Clint said. "You can see I'm not a detective."

"Roper tells me you have good instincts," Reno said. "Says he could make a detective out of you if you'd let him."

"Well, I've got a life," Clint said. "There are other things I'd rather do."

"I don't have a life," Reno said, "and this is all I do."

"Lots of people live for their work," Clint said. "Nothing wrong with that."

"I suppose not."

"Doesn't really leave much time for a personal life."

"That's okay," Reno said. "I don't need one."

"No wife? Girlfriend?"

"No," Reno said. "I know where to find a woman when I need one."

"Sounds like you've got your life figured out."

"To a certain extent," Reno said. "I've got it figured out now, but I don't know where I'm headed in the future."

"One day at a time is not a bad way to live."

After breakfast they walked out to the lobby together and shook hands.

"I'll get that information for you as soon as I can," Reno said. "And I'll keep taking the seven to seven shift at the hospital."

"Thanks, Joe."

"If you need anything else," Reno said, "just ask."

As Reno left, Clint thought he'd be suspicious of the man's eagerness to help if he hadn't been recommended by Tal Roper. That was probably just his own suspicious nature talking, though.

TWENTY-SIX

Clint was surprised that he was able to enter Rick Hartman's room so easily, but he was also surprised that he did not hear the man who came up behind him and pressed the barrel of his gun to the back of his head.

"You're not a doctor or a nurse, friend," a man's voice said, "so you better have a good reason for coming in here."

"Who is it?" Rick asked from the bed. "Who is that?"

"It's me, Rick."

"Take it easy, Stryker," Rick said. "You pull that trigger, you're going to have yourself a big rep as the man who killed Clint Adams."

The barrel of the gun was withdrawn from his head and Clint heard the hammer being released on a gun.

"Sorry, Mr. Adams," Andy Stryker said. "I was instructed to be careful."

"That's okay," Clint said. "Can I turn around, now?"

"Please."

He turned and found himself facing a rather genial-looking man as tall as he was, about ten years younger. The man holstered his gun and stuck out his hand.

"Pleased to meet you," Stryker said, as they shook hands.

"How's our patient doing?" Clint asked.

"You'll have to ask the doctor that. Don't think he'll be getting up anytime soon, though."

That sounded kind of harsh to Clint until Rick said, "I told him that, Clint."

Clint approached the bed.

"You satisfied with the security you're getting?" he asked.

"Yeah, Reno and Stryker seem to be pretty organized."

"Good." Clint turned to Stryker. "If you want to get a cup of coffee or a drink, Mr. Stryker, I can spell you a while."

"If it's all the same to you, sir," Stryker said, "I don't drink coffee, and I don't drink when I'm working."

"He's serious," Rick added.

"I guess so," Clint said, then looked at Stryker. "You can call me Clint, and do you prefer Andy, or Stryker?"

"Stryker's good," the man said.

"Okay, then."

"Clint, what have you found out so far?"

"I've talked to all the other potential buyers," Clint replied. "I think they're all capable of this, but especially Castle."

"Jake Castle?" Stryker asked.

Clint turned and looked at him.

"Yeah, he's here from New York to try to buy the Red Queen. Do you know him?"

"Ran into him in New York one time," Stryker said. "I didn't know he was in town."

"Did that run-in have to do with his business, or yours?" Clint asked.

"Both, I'm afraid."

"And the outcome?"

"Not good."

"For you or him?"

"Let's just say neither one of us would be happy to see the other again."

"I may be able to use you for more than just security, Stryker."

"As long as you can handle my fee."

"We'll talk about it."

Clint talked with Rick for a little while about Labyrinth, some of the people they both knew, and then about riding Duke part of the way to San Francisco.

"The big fella's here?" Rick asked.

"In a stable near the Red Queen," Clint said. "I'm going to go and check on him today, in fact."

"Be good to see him again, when I get back on my feet," Rick said, and then added, "Whenever that is."

"I'm sure the doctors will know something, soon."

"They tell you I can't feel my legs?" Rick asked.

"Um, yeah, they did."

"They tell you when that would change?"

Clint decided to be straight with his friend.

"The doctor said they wouldn't really know until some of the swelling went down."

"This is killing me, you know," Rick said, "just lying here like this."

"Yeah," Clint said, "I guess it would be killing me, too."

"So then why don't you get out there and find the jaspers who did this to me?" Rick asked. "You got me two baby-sitters, there's no need for you to keep coming by to keep me company."

"Just thought I'd drop in—"

"Drop in when you can tell me who pulled the trigger," Rick said. "You keep coming in here like this, you're going to mess up the routine Stryker and I have established."

Clint looked at Stryker, who shrugged helplessly.

"Okay, Rick," Clint said, "the next time you see me I'll have the names for you. How's that?"

"That sounds like a good deal, and it make it soon, huh?"

"Soon as I can."

He headed for the door, stopped when Rick said, "And Clint?"

"Yeah?"

"Thanks."

"Don't mention it."

TWENTY-SEVEN

The first shot came as soon as Clint walked out the front door of the hospital. It smacked into the door right next to his head. The second shot came a second later, but he had already launched himself off the steps in a dive. As he landed, he rolled and drew his gun. Several more shots and he quickly became aware that he was being fired at by at least three shooters.

He found cover behind a buggy that probably belonged to someone visiting a patient in the hospital. He peered across the street between the spokes of the wheel, trying to spot at least one shooter. If there were, indeed, three, then the prime suspects would be the three men from the casino. If they followed him to the hospital, he was going to feel like a fool for not spotting them.

Someone came out the front door of the hospital and drew fire from across the street. They ducked back inside but had already served Clint's purpose. He spotted two muzzle flashes and knew where two of the shooters were. They were secreted in two different doorways right across from the hospital.

Clint looked up at the hospital door and saw Andy Stryker peering out, gun in hand. He waved at Stryker to get back inside. What if this was a ruse to draw Stryker away from Rick's room?

Stryker peered out again and Clint felt he didn't have a choice.

"Get back inside!" he shouted.

"I count three shooters," Stryker called back.

"Get back to Rick's room. There should be some police here pretty soon."

Stryker waved that he understood and withdrew inside.

Clint wasn't sure if police would arrive. This was a city street, not Front Street in Tombstone, so presumably someone would think to call the police when they heard the shots being fired.

He decided he couldn't just lie there and wait. He was going to have to do something, and the only thing that made any sense was to draw their fire again, and give himself a shot back.

Eddy Squire crouched in his doorway across the street from the hospital and reloaded his gun. He didn't know who the other man was who had stuck his head out the front door, but he seemed to be gone. His two friends from the casino—Johnny Grad and Will Peters—were in their own doorways. The ambush had been their idea, but one of them had fired too damned soon and warned Adams they were there. Eddy had wanted to face Adams in the casino the night before, but his two partners had insisted on an ambush.

"He'll never know what hit him," Grad had said, "and then we claim the credit for killing the Gunsmith."

Now they'd missed and Adams had been alerted. What were they supposed to do now?

"Eddy, you see him?" Johnny Grad called from the next doorway.

"No. What about Will?"

"He don't see him, either."

"Fuck!" Eddy shouted. "We can't wait here forever."

"Is your door open?" Grad asked.

Eddy tried the door and found it locked. He looked in the window and saw that the place was deserted. He rattled the door to see how secure it was.

"It's locked, but I can force it."

"Okay," Johnny said, "we can cover Will while he moves to my doorway, and then you can cover us so we can get to yours. Then we force the door and try to find a back way out."

"We gonna run?" Eddy asked.

"He'll chase us," Johnny said, "and we can ambush him again."

"Yeah," Eddy said, under his breath, "like the first time worked so good."

"Ready?" Johnny called.

Clint knew the men were shouting back and forth but couldn't make out their words. He knew where they were, though, so he kept watch for them to make a move.

Suddenly, a man broke from a doorway that seemed to be farther down the street and ran to another one while two men fired at the front of the hospital. It became clear to him that they had no idea where he was.

The next time it was two men breaking from a doorway and one man trying to cover them. Clint got up, braced himself on the buggy, and fired twice. A bullet took one man in the back and the other lower down, possibly in the butt. The third man, alerted to where Clint was, began to fire at him, but the damage was done. Whatever the three men had been planning, two of them were now injured, one possibly dead.

Clint dropped down behind the buggy and replaced the spent rounds on his gun with live ones, so he'd be fully loaded.

• • •

Johnny Grad felt the bullet strike him in the back. He fell
into the doorway, Eddy ducking out of the way. Grad
struck the door so hard it slammed open, and he fell to
the floor.

When Clint's second bullet struck Will Peters in the
left buttock he cried out and stumbled against Johnny
Grad. It was their combined weight that snapped the door
open, causing them both to stumble into the empty store-
front.

"Christ!" Eddy said. "You guys all right?"

There was no answer, just the sound of groaning.

"Come on, get up, guys!"

Will Peters rolled off of Johnny Grad and that's when
Eddy saw the blood.

"Aw, man . . . are you both hit?"

Peters moaned, and Grad didn't make a sound.

Looked like the plans for a second ambush were going
to have to be changed.

There was little or no activity from the doorway, and Clint
was sure he'd killed one of the men, maybe both. He
decided a frontal attack was the best bet, now. He broke
from the cover of the buggy and ran across the street
without drawing fire. When he reached the other side he
flattened himself against a wall and waited. . . .

Eddy leaned over to check Peters, who was rolling around
holding his butt with both hands. His gun and Grad's were
both on the floor.

Quickly, he straightened and looked back across the
street. But he'd missed Clint's dash from behind the
buggy and thought he was still there. Angrily he fired
several shots in that direction when suddenly a hand
clamped down on his wrist and yanked him from the
doorway. . . .

•   •   •

Clint pulled Eddy from the doorway and clubbed him over the head with his gun. The man fell to the ground with a moan, unconscious. Clint stepped into the doorway, gun held out in front of him, and looked down at the two fallen men. He stepped over them and kicked their guns across the floor.

Covering them, he leaned over to check on both of them. One was dead, the other was lying on one side, holding his hands over his bleeding butt.

"You'll live," Clint said, "probably, but it's more than you deserve."

As he stood up a uniformed policeman appeared in the doorway, pointing a gun at him.

"Take it easy, Officer Bentley," he said to young Jed Bentley, "it's all over."

TWENTY-EIGHT

"They had nothing to do with the shooting of your friend," Lieutenant Rawlins said to Clint. "It was you they were after."

"I could have told you that," Clint replied.

He was sitting in the lieutenant's office. One man had been taken to the undertaker, the other to the hospital, and the third man—Eddy—had been arrested and was in a cell. Standing behind Clint and to his right was Officer Jed Bentley.

"Adams, you're lucky Officer Bentley, here, corroborates your story, or I'd have you in a cell right now."

"For what? Getting shot at?"

"For sticking your nose where it doesn't belong!"

"And where was that?"

"I don't want you running your own investigation into who shot Hartman," Rawlins said.

"I wasn't," Clint said. "I went there to visit him, and these three yahoos decided to ambush me. Like you said, it had nothing to do with Rick's shooting, so you've got no reason to put me in a cell."

Rawlins stared at Clint for a few moments, then looked past him at Bentley.

"Get him out of here," he finally said.

• • •

Bentley walked Clint outside and they stopped on the street in front of the police station.

"Thanks for your help," Clint said. "You probably kept me out of jail."

"I'm not always in agreement with Lieutenant Rawlins on his tactics," Bentley said.

"You don't get along with Rawlins?"

Bentley bit his lip, then said, "He's crooked. He upholds the law when it suits him, and bends it when it suits him."

"I'm sure he's not the only one, Jed."

"Well, I don't have to like it," Jed Bentley said. "Maybe it makes me naïve, but I'm never going to be like that."

"It makes you honest," Clint said, "and an honorable man. There's nothing wrong with either."

"Thank you, Mr. Adams," Bentley said. "My father told me there's been no change in Mr. Hartman's condition. I'm sorry."

"All we can do is hope for the best," Clint said. "I assume your father is a good doctor?"

The young man looked surprised, insisted, "He's a great doctor!" then realized Clint was just trying to get a rise out of him.

"If there's anything else I can do for you, please let me know," he said. They shook hands and parted company.

Before he left the hospital to accompany Rawlins to the police station, Clint had gone back inside to check on Rick. Nothing had happened during the short time Andy Stryker had been away from the room to see what was happening outside.

"I appreciate that you wanted to help," Clint told Stryker, "but it might have been a plan to get you away from

the room. In the future, don't leave that room for any
reason. Okay?"

"I understand," Stryker said. "You're the boss."

"Thank you."

With that Clint had accompanied Rawlins and Bentley . . .

When he got back to the hotel he went into the bar for a
drink. At midday there were plenty of tables and he had
his pick. As usual he took his beer to a table in a corner,
where he could sit with his back to the wall. It was a
normal precaution on his part, but seemed particularly
called for today.

He was only half done with the mug of beer when Joe
Reno appeared in the doorway. Clint waved at him to
come over, but the young man stopped at the bar for a
beer first. He came over, set it down on the table, and sat
opposite Clint.

"I heard what happened at the hospital today."

"Not at the hospital," Clint said. "In front. Nothing to
do with Rick Hartman's shooting."

"That may be, but maybe you need somebody to watch
your back," Reno said. "I could get somebody to do it, or
get a second man for the hospital and do it myself."

"I appreciate the offer, Joe, and I may take you up on
it later," Clint said. "Have you found out anything about
pros being in town?"

"No, nothing yet," Reno said. "There are plenty of men
with reps in town, but nobody who'd hire out for the kind
of money that was probably paid for this job."

"What makes you think you know how much was
paid?"

"Just considering the principals involved," Reno said.
"Jake Castle, a banker, a wealthy businessman, they'd pay
top dollar for a top name."

"Makes sense," Clint said, "as long as one of the three of them is involved."

"I thought you'd decided that, already."

"No," Clint said, "like I said, it makes sense, but there's always a chance it was someone else."

"Well, it wasn't a random robbery attempt."

"No."

"Jealous boyfriend, maybe?" Reno asked. "Was he seeing someone here in town?"

"Actually," Clint replied, "he was, and that's something I haven't asked her yet. Thanks."

"Well, once you've eliminated that, and robbery, you'll only have to eliminate someone with a grudge seeing him and acting on impulse. Once you do that, you're left with the other three principals who are vying for the hotel."

"You see?" Clint said. "That's why I say I'm not a detective. Thanks for your insight, Joe."

"Consider it part of the service," Reno said. "Well, I better get home and catch my four hours."

"I'll walk you as far as the bar," Clint said. "I'm going to have another drink."

"Um, I told the bartender I was with you, and he didn't charge me. Shall I pay you—"

"Forget it," Clint said. "I'm a guest of the owner."

They walked as far as the bar together and then Reno said good-bye and left. Clint got himself another beer and took it back to the table with him. He was glad Reno had come in when he did, because he hadn't at all been sure about his next step.

Jealous boyfriend. Why hadn't he thought of that?

TWENTY-NINE

Clint spent a good two hours trying to catch up with Grace Morgan, who seemed to be a very busy woman. She wasn't in her office, in the dining room, anywhere else in the hotel, or in the casino. Finally he went to the front desk to talk to the desk clerk. This one was a new one, a third name for him to remember.

"Jason, sir," the man answered. He was older than the other two clerks, about sixty.

"I'd like to leave a message for Miss Morgan."

"Yes, sir," Jason said. "My pleasure. What is the message?"

"Would you ask her to meet me in the dining room for dinner about . . . oh, seven?"

"Miss Morgan doesn't usually dine until eight, sir."

"Okay, make it eight o'clock."

"Yes, sir."

"You're very efficient, Jason."

"Thank you, sir."

"And if you don't mind me saying so, you seem better at your job than the others."

"They're young, sir," Jason said. "I'm doing my best with them."

"Thanks, Jason."

"You're welcome, sir."

Clint walked away from the desk, decided to go to his room to clean up after rolling in the street that morning avoiding lead.

Jake Castle opened the door to his room and saw both Wayne Jackson, the businessman, and Edward O'Brien, the banker.

"Gentlemen," he said, backing away so they could enter, "thank you for accepting my invitation to have a drink in my room."

"Why here and not the bar, Castle?" O'Brien asked. "Are you ashamed to be seen with legitimate businessmen?" The older man was smiling, but there was still suspicion in his words. Neither he nor Jackson considered Jake Castle to be a legitimate businessman. That was something Castle knew he'd make them regret, sooner or later.

"I don't think we should be seen together in public," Castle said. "Not with Clint Adams conducting his investigation."

"He's spoken to you, then?" Jackson asked.

"He's spoken to all of us, I think," Castle said. "He's convinced that one of us is behind the shooting of his friend, Rick Hartman."

"You said something about a drink," Jackson said, scowling.

"Whiskey okay?" Castle asked.

"I prefer it," Jackson said.

"So do I," Ed O'Brien said.

Castle poured out three large whiskeys and handed them out.

"All right, Castle," O'Brien said, taking charge—he thought, "what's on your mind?"

"I was wondering, gentlemen," Castle said, "which of you had Hartman shot?"

Jackson choked on his whiskey while O'Brien just gaped at Jake Castle.

"You've got nerve, man!" the banker said. "I think it's pretty clear to everyone in this room that you are the one behind that business."

"Me?" Castle asked. "Why would I want the man shot?"

Jackson cleared his throat and, after a sip of whiskey, said, "Excuse us, but isn't that what you do, sir? Shoot people?"

"You should both know that if I want someone shot," Castle said, "I do it myself. I face a man and pump a bullet into his gut, I don't backshoot from cover. No, one of you had this done. You hired it out, and I tell you, I really don't care. We all know Hartman was the front-runner to buy this hotel and casino from Miss Morgan. Now that he's out of the way one of us can make the purchase."

"Let me get this straight," O'Brien said. "You asked us to come here so you could accuse us of having a man shot, and then tell us that you don't care?"

"I called you here to warn you," Castle said. "I know Clint Adams well. He's not going to let go of this. Whichever one of you did this, make sure your tracks are covered, and make sure your shooter leaves San Francisco."

"This is excellent whiskey," Jackson said, "but not good enough to put up with this drivel. Good day, sir."

Wayne Jackson stormed from the room, leaving Castle and O'Brien facing each other.

"You're still here," Castle said. "That means either you did it, or you believe he did."

"Actually," O'Brien said, "I thought all along that you did it, but Jackson could have hired it out."

"But you didn't do it?"

"Of course not."

"Then why are you still here?"

O'Brien smiled and said, "Mr. Jackson was right about one thing."

"What was that?"

"This whiskey," the banker said. "It really is excellent."

"Would you like another glass?"

"Yes, very much," O'Brien said, handing his glass to his host, "and then maybe you and I can do some business, Mr. Castle."

"Well," Jake Castle said, handing O'Brien another whiskey, "that does sound interesting. Tell me, Mr. O'Brien, what do you have in mind?"

THIRTY

After a bath and a change of clothes Clint decided to kill some time in the casino. He still had five hundred dollars of Grace Morgan's money to play with.

It was getting on toward evening when he entered the casino and the tables were beginning to fill up. He saw Wayne Jackson sitting at the same blackjack table as the day before. In fact, he was in the same chair, the second one.

Clint walked over to the table, sat down at the fifth and last chair and bought some chips from the dealer. When Wayne Jackson heard his voice he looked up at him, and seemed startled.

" 'Evening, Mr. Jackson," Clint said. He inclined his head to indicate the stacks of chips in front of the businessman. "Seems you're doing quite well for yourself, tonight."

"I am on a bit of a winning streak," Jackson said. "Is, uh, blackjack your game, sir?"

"Not really," Clint said, "but I just thought I'd pass some time with a few hands. You don't mind, do you?"

"I don't own the place," Jackson said, then added, "yet."

"You sound confident."

"There's no point in doing business if you're not confident," Jackson said. "I'm sure you find the same true in your life."

"Oh, yes," Clint said, nodding in agreement. "Confidence is a very important thing." On the other hand, overconfidence was not a good thing, and that was what the businessman was dealing in.

The dealer dealt them each two cards. Jackson took a hit and busted. Clint had a king face down and a four up. The dealer was showing a six and was going to have to take a hit.

"I stand," he said, surprising Jackson, who had drawn to his own sixteen. Clint had made the intelligent play, Jackson the foolish one. The man may have considered blackjack his game, but it was plain that he either didn't know the rudiments of it, or didn't care. His play seemed based on his feelings, and Clint wondered if he did business the same way. Maybe his instincts served him well in his everyday life, but certainly not in gambling.

The dealer flipped his down card, which was a face card worth ten. He did indeed have sixteen.

"House hits on sixteen," the man said, and flipped another picture card, "and busts. Pay fourteen."

He paid Clint while Jackson fumed. If he'd stood he would have been getting paid, too.

For the next hour Jackson's luck went south while Clint kept winning. If Clint had been in the man's shoes he would have quit as soon as his luck went bad, but Jackson kept pounding away, sending good money after bad, splitting tens almost every time, which meant he was throwing away winning hands to chase two winning hands.

By the time Grace Morgan put in an appearance Wayne Jackson's collar was open and he was sweating. The stack of chips Clint had commented on was gone, and he had bought additional chips twice more. His betting was becoming more and more reckless.

"Gentlemen," she said, standing between them. "I hope you're both winning."

"Well," Clint said, "Mr. Jackson was winning when I got here, but now it seems he's losing. I hope my presence wasn't enough to affect your concentration and break your streak, sir?"

Jackson got off his stool and straightened his collar. He turned to Grace Morgan.

"I'm afraid I need to take a break," Jackson said. "If you'll excuse me?"

"Of course."

As Jackson stalked off, Grace turned to Clint and asked, "What did you do to that man?"

"Gave him a blackjack lesson, if you ask me," the dealer said, with a grin. "Mr. Adams knows the rules, and Mr. Jackson keeps trying to make his own."

"Barry," Grace said, pushing Clint's chips toward the dealer, "cash Mr. Adams in, please. He's going to take me to dinner."

Clint noticed that Grace was dressed for work in another spangled gown with a plunging neckline.

"Do you usually dress this well to eat in your own dining room?" he asked.

"Oh no," she said, "you invited me to dinner, so we're not eating here, we're going out."

Clint looked down at his own clothes which, while clean, were certainly not what you'd call evening clothes.

"Don't worry," she said, "I have a place picked out where you'll fit right in."

"Your money, sir."

Clint had doubled his winnings and was back up to a thousand dollars. This time instead of making a magnanimous gesture by tipping the dealer half his winnings he plucked fifty dollars from his poke and handed it to Barry.

"Thank you, sir."

"Thank you, Barry."

Clint pocketed his money, then turned to Grace and extended his arm.

"Madam? Time for dinner?"

"Why, thank you, sir," she said, slipping her arm into his.

They walked out of the casino that way.

THIRTY-ONE

Grace chose a restaurant that was in Portsmouth Square between two large hotels. It was dinnertime, but the maitre d' obviously knew her and conducted them to a regular table.

The people in the place were a mixed group, from two men who looked like they'd just come off the range to another couple who were apparently dressed for the theater.

"You come here a lot?" Clint asked.

"Quite a bit, yes," she said. "Especially when I want to get away from the Red Queen."

"You come here alone?"

She raised her eyebrows.

"That's a personal question."

He shrugged and said, "Then don't answer it."

"No, no," she said, "that's okay. Yes, sometimes I come alone, and sometimes I come with friends."

"Men friends?"

"I have a few men friends, yes."

"So, with Rick warning me away from you, does he know about your other friends?"

"I never told Rick he was the only man I was sleeping

131

with," Grace explained. "He was the newest man I was sleeping with."

"I see. So I guess he was taking this relationship a little more seriously than you were."

"A lot more."

A waiter came over and they ordered dinner and drinks. Clint took the time to study Grace Morgan. He could understand what his friend saw in her. She was beautiful, and she was in the same business as he was. He probably saw them running a hotel and casino somewhere together.

"When were you planning on telling him this?"

"I was enjoying myself, Clint," she said. "I didn't see any reason to bring it up. Rick strikes me as the kind of man who would have stopped sleeping with me."

"I think you're right."

"So, no, I wasn't ready to tell him, yet. However, I think I'll have to tell him as soon as he's back on his feet."

"That would seem like a good idea."

"And what about you?"

"What about me?"

"Any special friends?"

"One or two."

"Like Brandy?" She raised one eyebrow when she asked that question.

"Tell me," Clint said, changing the subject, "when were you going to make your decision about who to sell to?"

"I don't know."

"Why do I get the feeling," Clint said, "that you like pitting men against each other?"

She laughed. "Men are so easy."

"In what way?"

"In every way," she said. "They're so eager to make fools of themselves over what a woman can give them."

"What's that got to do with business?"

The waiter came with their drinks, set them down, and

walked away, promising to return soon with their dinners. When he was gone Grace went right back to the question.

"How much attention do you think men like these would pay me if I didn't have something they wanted?"

"According to you, women always have something men want," he reminded her.

"In this case, I commanded some respect from businessmen because of what I owned," she said, "not because of how I looked."

"So you decided to take advantage of this and make them jump through hoops?"

She smiled and said, "Exactly."

"I have to admire your honesty."

"I love honesty," she said, "and I would have been honest with Rick—in fact, I was honest with him. I told him we were having fun, and I never discussed anything permanent with him."

Clint frowned. Rick Hartman was not a man who was waiting for the right woman to come along and make him happy. He was always happy with what he had, until he suddenly announced he was going to leave Labyrinth and open a place in San Francisco. Maybe if he was ready for a change like that, he was also ready for a woman to be in his life. If he had decided that Grace Morgan was that woman, he had apparently made a mistake.

Suddenly, she sat forward, reached out, and covered his hand with hers.

"Now that we've established how honest I am, what about you?" she asked.

"Meaning what?"

"Meaning wouldn't you like to get me out of this dress and do things to my naked body?"

"Under normal circumstances the answer would be yes."

"And what keeps this from being a normal circumstance?"

"I think you know."

She sat back.

"We've established that I'm not going to marry Rick Hartman," she said, "even if he decides to ask me. I don't see what the problem is."

"Rick asked me to stay away from you," Clint said, "and that's what I intend to do."

She regarded him across the table for a moment, then picked up her fork. "In that case, this meal is going to become even more expensive for you."

THIRTY-TWO

Over a very expensive dessert Clint asked Grace about the other men in her life.

"What about them?"

"Would any of them be jealous enough to shoot Rick down in the street?"

She hesitated, taking a moment to drink some of her wine.

"Is that a difficult question?" he asked.

"I'm counting," she said.

"Counting . . . what?"

"Men."

"Are there that many?"

She grinned and said, "Always room for one more."

"Grace . . ."

"Why is it men can sleep with as many women as they want," she said, "go to whorehouses and sleep with dozens, but when a woman does it—"

"I don't care how many men you sleep with," Clint said. "I only care if one of them is shooting my friends."

She finished her dessert—something very chocolate—and used a cloth napkin to clean her mouth before she answered.

"I don't think any of my men friends would have a reason or an inclination to have Rick shot. For one thing, Rick is a temporary thing."

"And the others?"

"Several of them are . . . permanent fixtures in my life."

"Permanent like marriage?" he asked, wondering if she had a husband somewhere. Whatever she claimed, a husband would be that jealous.

"Well," she said, "not married to me."

"So most of your male friends are already married?"

"Yes," she said. "It makes things much, much simpler."

"What if one of them wanted to divorce his wife and marry you?" he asked.

"Oh no," she said, "that wouldn't happen."

"Why not?"

"I wouldn't allow it," she said. "For one thing, if they're cheating on their wives with me, why wouldn't they cheat on me if I married one of them?"

"Maybe they wouldn't have to cheat once they were with you?" he suggested.

"Clint," she said. "If I've learned one thing about men it's that it doesn't matter who they're married to, they have to cheat."

"All men?" he asked.

"All men," she said, "are cheaters."

He sat back in his chair and stared at her.

"You don't agree?"

"No," he said. "I know a lot of men who are happily married."

"That's crap," she said. "I don't know any happily married men."

"You have a very jaded view of the world, Grace."

"It serves me well," she said. "It will keep me from ever getting hurt."

"Again?"

"What?"

"I just had the feeling that the word 'again' belonged at the end of that sentence."

She finished her wine and set the glass down hard.

"Yes, all right," she said, "I've been hurt in the past. Who hasn't? But I'll never be hurt again."

"Not as long as you're the one doing the hurting."

"I'm not hurting anyone."

"The wives of the men you're seeing?"

"Being with me sends them back to their wives very happy."

"Well," Clint said, "I think this game you're playing with the Red Queen is what got Rick shot."

"You can't blame me for that," she said. "I'm waiting for him to recover before I make my decision."

"Why?"

"Why?" she repeated. "I'm being fair to him."

"No you're not," he said. "You're still making these men dance to your tune. It has nothing to do with being fair to Rick. I'm sure you've heard everyone's offer by now, and have enough information to base your decision on. You're just not done playing games."

"Well, I'll tell you something I am done with," she said, "and that's dinner. Would you walk me back to the hotel, please?"

"Sure," he said. "Just let me pay the check and we can be on our way."

"What was this about?" she asked, as they walked back.

"I needed to know if you had any jealous suitors," he said. "I think I got more than I bargained for."

"Most men do when they deal with me."

"I can believe that."

When they reached the hotel Grace turned to him and extended her hand formally.

"Thank you for dinner."

"You're welcome."

"Clint, I am very sorry that Rick was hurt," she said. "I hope you find the men who did it."

"Don't worry," he said, "I will."

She stared at him for a moment, then said, "I believe you . . . and I feel sorry for them when you do."

As she walked away Clint hoped that it was a man who responsible, and not a woman.

THIRTY-THREE

The next morning Jake Castle awoke with the whore down between his legs. She was high priced, and good at what she did. She'd taken him to the limit during the night, and now she was sucking on his erect penis like it was some tasty candy stick.

He'd sent for the girl after Edward O'Brien had left this room the previous evening. Castle and the banker had come to an agreement that seemed mutually convenient. Of course, the banker would find out different later, but for now they were partners.

The girl had him going good, now, his butt lifting up off the bed. She slid her hands beneath him to cup his ass in her hands as he exploded into her mouth with a loud, guttural moan. . . .

Castle tossed some bills at the girl when she finished dressing and said, "Get out."

"Again tonight?" she asked.

He studied her for a woman. Long and lean the way he liked them, but her face was too hard and she was at least forty. She'd been at this too long.

"I don't think so," he said. "I think I need someone

prettier tonight. Don't get me wrong, you're good, but you're just too damn ugly."

"Wha—".

"Get out!" he snapped. "You got your money, now get the hell out."

Close to tears, the whore rushed from the room. Castle thought she should have had a thicker skin for someone who had obviously been in the business a long time.

He decided to take a bath and wash the smell of her off of him. . . .

Banker O'Brien woke and rolled out of bed, his back aching as it usually did when he wasn't sleeping in his own bed. His meeting last night with Jake Castle had gone well. The New York gangster actually believed that they were partners. As if O'Brien would ever really be partners with the likes of him. The man had actually offered to send a whore to O'Brien's room. The man had been married to the same woman for thirty years and loved her dearly. What would he need with a diseased whore?

What he really needed was a long hot bath to soothe his aching back. . . .

Wayne Jackson hated to admit it, but he was out of his element. He did not feel comfortable dealing with men like Jake Castle and Clint Adams. They were both killers, you could see it in their eyes. The Red Queen was certainly not worth getting killed over. And with O'Brien staying behind to talk with Castle last night, it seemed as if those two might form an alliance. And he wasn't doing well at blackjack, thanks to Clint Adams. The man had trampled all over his luck.

No, it was time for Wayne Jackson to give it up and head home. He was not destined to be the new owner of the Red Queen Hotel. . . .

•   •   •

Grace Morgan was still seething when she woke the next morning. She thought a good night's sleep would ease the sting of being rejected by Clint Adams—twice—but, if anything, it was worse.

She'd never wanted a man in her bed more, and it was a distraction she didn't need. There was business to finish, and Clint may have been right. Waiting for Rick to recover might not have been such a good idea. Still, she certainly felt she owed it to Rick to let him know that she was going to go ahead and make her decision.

But not until she'd had a bath, and maybe imagined that Clint Adams was in there with her. . . .

When Clint woke alone he wished he had a woman with him. Not Grace, though. He was thinking about Brandy. She would have warmed his bed just right last night. Not that Grace Morgan wouldn't be a wild woman in bed. He knew that she would. She had to be if she was keeping so many men happy. But Clint didn't like sharing a woman, especially not with more than one man—and definitely not when one of those men was Rick Hartman.

As he rose from bed he wondered if he should tell Rick about Grace's other men. Or maybe he already knew. Rick was a smart man, but he was smarter when it came to business than when it came to women. Of course, making him feel foolish while he was lying flat on his stomach didn't seem like such a good idea. Better to let him recover first.

He'd learned at the dinner the previous night that Grace Morgan was an unusual woman—maybe a bit too unusual for him. Certainly too complicated, and making up for some early pain in her life. He had his own problems and didn't need to have a woman in his life who had her own, as well. He was too busy—or selfish—dealing with his own.

There was no way he was going to end up in her bed, no matter how desirable she was. That was where Brandy would come in. She'd help keep him too busy to wonder what he might be missing.

THIRTY-FOUR

When Joe Reno got the word about who was in town he was stunned. He wasn't impressed with many men. Clint Adams was certainly one of them, as well as Talbot Roper. However, gunmen who sold themselves to the highest bidder usually didn't impress him—except for this man.

It was early in the morning when he got the word. He'd returned home from being at the hospital all night, and someone was waiting for him outside his rooms.

He got the word, and immediately headed for the Red Queen Hotel to fill Clint in.

Clint was coming out of the dining room after having breakfast when he saw Joe Reno enter the hotel. Reno spotted him and immediately rushed over to him.

"I've got something for you."

"Great," Clint said. "You want to get some coffee—"

"Let's take a walk."

"Fine."

They left the hotel and walked away from Portsmouth Square, rather than toward it.

"What's this about?"

"I got the word today about somebody who's been seen in town," Reno said.

"And?"

"And I can't say that he's the shooter," Reno said, "but he's certainly hired out before."

Clint put his hand on Reno's arm to stop him from walking any farther.

"Who are we talking about, Joe?"

"Do you know a man called Reverend Jim?"

Clint rubbed his jaw.

"I knew a gunman called Preacher, once," Clint said. "Seems Reverend sounds familiar, too."

"It should," Reno said. "He's about the fastest thing around, if you put any stock in reputations."

"Personally, I don't," Clint said wryly. "How long has Reverend Jim been plying his trade?"

"A few years now," Reno said. "His rep has grown very quickly."

"Wait a minute," Clint said. "Central City, a couple of years ago? Killed . . . what. Six men?"

"Seven," Reno said. "Middle of the street, no cover. Just took them all down."

"One gun or two?" Clint asked, only half serious.

"Two," Reno said.

"Sounds like a penny dreadful, Joe."

"It happened."

"How do you know?"

"I was there," Reno said, and then started walking again.

Suddenly Reno ran into the street and hailed a passing cab. He gave the driver instructions to take them to the Barbary Coast.

"Why are we going to the Coast?" Clint asked.

"Let's talk about it when we get there," Reno said, and would not say another word until they arrived.

*   *   *

The Bucket of Blood Saloon hadn't changed since the last time Clint was there, which was . . . well, he couldn't remember. When they entered, Reno went to the bar, exchanged a few words with a bartender who wore an eye patch, then got two beers and beckoned Clint to join him at a back table.

"Okay," Clint said, "why are we drinking watered-down beer on the Barbary Coast when we could be drinking the good stuff in Portsmouth Square?"

"Because we're not going to find out about Reverend Jim in Portsmouth Square."

"Joe, tell me again about Central City."

"I was there, doing a job that had nothing to do with Reverend Jim," Reno said, "but there he was, sporting a long black duster, two guns, and a crucifix around his neck."

"Sounds pretty theatrical."

"But effective. Men stepped aside to let him by. Women shied away from him, even though he'd doff his hat and say good day. Clint, Reverend Jim was the scariest man I'd ever seen."

"You were younger then," Clint said, joking again, but Reno seemed to take everything he said seriously.

"You're right, I was," the younger man said. "I've seen a few things since then, and I'm not as easily impressed as I was, but Reverend Jim is different."

"Well, it doesn't sound like he can blend in with the background," Clint said. "Why would he come here for a high-profile job like shooting a man down in the street spitting distance from the square?"

"Money," Reno said. "The Reverend is expensive, and only takes a few jobs a year."

"A man who could face six in the street and kill them fair and square," Clint said, "why would he backshoot a man?"

"I don't know," Reno said. "I don't know that he took

the job, I only know that he's been seen in town."

"Well, maybe we won't have to deal with him, then," Clint said. "Shooting Rick down doesn't sound like the kind of job he'd take."

"You don't get it, do you?" Reno asked.

"Get what?"

"Shooting Rick may not be the kind of job he'd take," Reno said, "but facing you . . . there's a job that would suit him, don't you think?"

THIRTY-FIVE

"Wait a minute," Clint said, "you think Reverend Jim is here for me?"

"Why else would he be here?" Reno asked. "There's nobody else in San Francisco worthy of his talents."

"You don't know that."

"Trust me, Clint," Reno said, "if Bat Masterson or Wyatt Earp or Ben Thompson were in town, I'd know."

"I've only been here a couple of days," Clint said. "No one could have gotten him here that quick."

"I checked," Reno said. "Hartman sent you that telegram weeks ago. Somebody could have brought the Reverend in, in anticipation of your arrival."

"Why would they think I'd come?"

"Maybe you don't know your own reputation."

"Only too well, believe me."

"Oh yeah? The part about coming to a friend's aid, no matter what?"

"That's part of my reputation?" Clint asked.

"A big part."

"Well," Clint said, "that's not such a bad reputation to have, is it?"

"I don't think we should be worried about your

reputation, right now," Reno said. "We should be worried about it coming to an end. You need somebody to watch your back."

"What'd you talk to the bartender about?"

"Whether or not Reverend Jim had been in here."

"Why would he come to this hole?"

"You know a place in town that might have more sinners?"

"Wait a minute," Clint said. "He's a real reverend?"

"Yep, and he likes his preaching. He'd come here to save as many souls as he could."

"Has he been in?"

"Not yet."

"And do you intend to sit here until he does?"

"I thought—"

"I have to find out who shot Rick, Joe," Clint said. "I can't be sitting here all day waiting for a man who might not arrive. And I can't drink this beer."

"I can sit and wait."

"You have a job, already," Clint said. "Besides, if he walks in what are you going to do? Ask him if he's here to kill me?"

"I hadn't thought it out that far," Reno said.

"Look," Clint said, pushing the flat, watered-down beer away, "I appreciate your concern for me, but you've got a job to do, and so do I. If Reverend Jim comes for me, he's going to come straight on, where I can see him. If that happens, I'll deal with it then."

"You think you can take him?" Reno asked. "I mean . . . he's, uh, younger, and . . . uh . . ."

"And I've been around a while?"

"Well, I didn't mean . . ."

"Believe me, Joe," Clint said, "this old-timer has some mileage left in him."

"Clint, I didn't mean . . ."

Clint stood up and said, "I'm going back to the hotel.

If you do happen to find out something, let me know. And keep your ears open in case some other gun for hire is spotted in town. Maybe somebody whose price isn't as high as the Reverend's."

"I'll do that," Reno said, "but I still think you ought to have someone watching—"

"Why is Reverend Jim's price so high, anyway?" Clint asked, cutting him off.

"Well," Reno said, "the story goes he's saving his money to build himself a church."

Clint thought about that a moment, then said, "Well, if that happened, at least it would keep him from traveling as much, wouldn't it?"

After Clint left, Joe Reno got up and walked to the bar.

"Another one?" the bartender asked.

"No," Reno said.

"Was that him?" the man asked. "Was that the Gunsmith?"

"Sam," Reno said, "I still want to hear if you see Reverend Jim in here, understand?"

Sam nodded and his one eye widened.

"Imagine that?" he asked. "The Gunsmith against the Reverend? Wouldn't that be something?"

"Yeah, it would."

"Where would you put your money, Joe?" Sam the bartender asked. "Then Gunsmith or the Reverend?"

Reno paused to consider the question. The Gunsmith had been around a long time, and to be around that long he had to be good. But Reno had never seen the Gunsmith in action. He had, however, seen Reverend Jim gun down six men in the street in Central City, Colorado. It had been the single most impressive thing he'd ever seen.

"I'd probably put my last dime," he said, "on the Reverend."

"Even with the rep the Gunsmith's got?" Sam asked. "My money would be on him."

"Yeah, well," Reno said. "Maybe it won't happen."

"Be somethin' if it did, though."

"Yeah," Reno said, and left the saloon.

THIRTY-SIX

"Are we set?" the banker, O'Brien, asked Castle.

"My man is here," Jake Castle said, regarding the older man across the table. They were in the Red Queen's dining room, where both men had taken all their meals since they first arrived in San Francisco.

"In the hotel?"

"In San Francisco."

"How did you get him here so fast?"

Castle smiled.

"He's been here a week," he said. "I sent for him a while back. He's just been waiting to hear from me."

"Are you sure this is what we have to do?"

"How badly do you want this hotel, banker?"

"Bad," O'Brien said. "It's a toehold into the square, after all, and that's where I want to go next."

The banker had big plans, which included owning more than one hotel and casino in Portsmouth Square. Personally, Castle would be satisfied with this one hotel, the Red Queen. And he wouldn't have minded having Grace Morgan along with it. He had never seen a classier woman in his life. He wondered if he could get a whore for the night who looked like her. He'd have to ask the desk clerk,

Jason. He was the man with all the connections.

"I've never done this before," O'Brien said.

"Done what?"

"Hired one man to kill another."

"It's nothing," Castle said. "It's a business decision, like any other. With Clint Adams around, this deal is not going to get done."

"Perhaps not . . ." O'Brien's voice trailed off as he looked past Castle, who turned in his seat. Wayne Jackson was walking toward them.

"Well, well," Castle said, as the man reached them, "the businessman is back."

"I only came to tell you I'm leaving," Jackson said. "I've checked out."

"Of the hotel?" Castle asked. "Or the whole deal."

"The entire deal," Jackson said. "You men can have the hotel. You obviously want it more than I do."

"I'm glad you can concede that, Mr. Jackson," O'Brien said.

"What made you come to that decision?" Castle asked.

Jackson looked at the two men and said, "You, Hartman, now Clint Adams . . . I think you're all crazy."

Rather than be offended, Jake Castle laughed, surprising both Jackson and O'Brien.

"You probably are right, Wayne," Castle said. "Have a nice trip home."

Jackson started to leave, then stopped and looked at Edward O'Brien.

"If I were you," he said, "I'd be careful of this man . . . very careful."

"We'll give your regards to Miss Morgan," Castle said.

"Yes," Jackson said. "Do that."

He turned and left the dining room, and the hotel.

"He's right, you know," Castle said to O'Brien.

"About us wanting this hotel more than he did?" the banker asked. "Yes, I believe he was."

"No, not that," Castle said.

O'Brien looked at him.

"About all of us being crazy?" he asked. "Well, I wouldn't go that far—"

"No," Castle said, "the other part, about you being very, very careful."

O'Brien frowned, wondering what Castle was trying to tell him.

"It's good advice," Jake Castle said, picking up his coffee cup, "always good advice."

O'Brien wondered if it wouldn't be the smart thing to do to just get up and follow Wayne Jackson out. But instead of doing that he asked, "So when will this be done?"

THIRTY-SEVEN

As Clint was stepping out of a cab, Wayne Jackson came rushing out of the hotel, waving his arm.

"Got another passenger for you," Clint said, noticing that Jackson was carrying a suitcase.

"I see 'im," the driver said, stepping down. "Just gonna get my horse some water."

"Can you take me to the train station?" Jackson asked the driver.

"Climb in, be with you in a minute."

"Leaving so soon, Mr. Jackson?" Clint asked.

Jackson looked at Clint as if he was only just recognizing him.

"Yes," Jackson said, "I've decided to pull out of this deal."

"Really? Why?"

"It's getting too complicated," the man said, "and too dangerous. Frankly, Mr. Adams, you scare me."

Clint studied the man's eyes and decided that Jackson was telling the truth. He also decided right there and then that the man didn't have the sand to have hired a shooter to kill Rick Hartman.

"Well, Mr. Jackson," he said, "I suppose that was my

intention. Now, if I could just scare one of the others into telling me which one hired the gunman—"

"If I were you, sir," Jackson said, climbing into the back of the cab, "I would be very careful of Mr. Castle and Mr. O'Brien."

"And why is that?"

"It seems to me they have formed some sort of unholy alliance," Jackson said. "Joined forces, as it were."

"And they didn't invite you?"

"Actually," he said, "they did, but I'm choosing to leave."

"Have you told Miss Morgan?"

"No," the businessman said. "I just spoke to both Castle and O'Brien in the dining room. They will pass on my decision to her, I'm sure."

"Yes, I'm sure they will."

The driver finished watering his horse, climbed aboard and drove off with Wayne Jackson.

One down, two to go, Clint thought, and went into the hotel.

When Clint entered the lobby he saw Jake Castle at the front desk, talking with Jason. As he watched, he was sure that money changed hands before Castle walked away. O'Brien was nowhere to be seen in the lobby. Clint waited a few minutes, then approached the front desk himself.

"Good afternoon, Mr. Adams," Jason said. "What can I do for you, today?"

"Jason," Clint said, "it strikes me that you might be the man in this hotel with all the answers."

"You flatter me, Mr. Adams," the man said. "I'm sure I don't even know all the questions."

"Oh, sure you do," Clint said. "Girls, a private game, something a little bit on the wrong side of the law. You've got the answers for a price, don't you?"

Jason hesitated, then said, "Well, someone has to."

"Exactly. I just saw Mr. Castle hand you some money. What was that for?"

Jason frowned.

"You won't tell Miss Morgan, will you, sir?"

"This is just between you and me, Jason."

"He wants a woman for the evening."

"Is that all?"

"Well . . . he wants her to look like Miss Morgan."

"Ah, I see," Clint said. "And can you deliver?"

"I think I can come close, sir."

"And are there any other special needs you've been meeting for the potential owners?"

"No, sir," Jason said. "Mr. Castle is the only one who has had special needs."

"All right, Jason," Clint said. "Thank you."

"If you need anything special, sir," the clerk said, "you just need to let me know."

"I'll keep that in mind."

Sam the bartender—who had lost his eye years ago to a boat hook as a teenager in a fight on the Barbary Coast docks—couldn't believe he'd had the Gunsmith himself in the saloon earlier that day. He knew Joe Reno was impressed by Reverend Jim, but that was a young man being impressed with a young man. Sam was older, in his forties, and he remembered all the stories he'd heard over the years about the Gunsmith. If only half of them were right then the Reverend Jim was no match for Clint Adams.

Still, when the man entered the Bucket of Blood Saloon only hours after Clint Adams had left, a shiver ran through Sam. Reverend Jim was a dark, gaunt figure with haunted eyes, and as he approached the bar Sam had to look right into those eyes.

"Whiskey, sinner," Reverend Jim said.

"Comin' up."

The Reverend downed the whiskey quickly and then said, "Now a beer."

"You got it."

The dark man paused to look around the place, found it mostly empty.

"When do the sinners arrive?" he asked, accepting the mug of beer.

"Any time, now," Sam said.

The Reverend turned his eyes onto Sam again, who was gripped by the urge to shrink away from them.

"And are you a sinner?" the man asked.

"I—I suppose."

"It looks to me like you might have given up an eye for your sins."

Sam's hand went to his eye patch.

"I changed my eye after I lost the eye," he said. "Now I own this place."

"And you serve watered-down whiskey and watered-down beer," Reverend Jim said. The brim of his hat shadowed his eyes, which seemed to shine from the shadows like fire.

"Uh, I, uh, I'm tryin' to make a livin'," Sam said. "I can get you a better mug of beer, if you want."

"No need," the other man said. "I will drink what the sinners drink, for how else can I deserve the right to preach to them, and save their souls?"

"I, uh, don't know . . ."

"Give me another," Jim said. "I'll take it to a table and wait for the sinners to arrive."

"Yes, sir."

Sam watched the Reverend Jim carry his second watered-down beer to a table. The man removed his flat-brimmed black hat, revealing long hair that hung to his shoulders, but a bald crown. It didn't seem that the gunman was a threat to him, but if he did become one, the bartender felt he still had an ace in the hole to play.

THIRTY-EIGHT

Clint went from the hotel to the hospital to talk to both Rick and Andy Stryker.

"So Jackson's gone and the other two have joined forces?" Rick asked.

"That's the way it looks."

"You know," Rick said, "I'm so damned tired of laying here I'm ready to go back to Labyrinth."

"And give up the life of a San Francisco hotel owner?" Clint asked.

"Right now, Rick's Place looks pretty good."

Clint looked at Stryker.

"I don't know what Castle and the banker joining up really means, so be extra careful."

"You got it."

"Rick, I'll see you soon."

"Watch your back, Clint. I want to go back to Labyrinth, but I also want to know that you will, too."

"Don't worry, partner," Clint said. "We'll both be going."

Stryker walked him to the door of the room and out into the hall.

"How many guns have you got?" Clint asked.

"Enough."

"Good."

Clint started away, then stopped short as he heard not only Rick Hartman's voice in his head, but Joe Reno's, as well. They were both saying "Watch your back," which seemed to be very good advice, especially with Rick lying in the hospital with a bullet wound in his back.

"Stryker, you know where Joe Reno lives?"

"Sure."

"Will you tell me?"

"Why not?" And he did, complete with directions.

"I may be bringing somebody else in to relieve you," Clint said.

"You gonna use Joe to watch your back?"

"I think it would be a good idea."

"Sounds good to me."

"The man I send to relieve you might be a policeman," Clint said. "Is that okay with you?"

"You're the boss. What's his name?"

"Bentley, like the doctor, here."

Stryker nodded. "Okay. I'll watch for him."

"Thanks."

Stryker went back into the room and Clint went in search of Doctor Bentley.

He was directed to an office and found the doctor seated behind his desk. As he entered he wondered if Doctor Bentley was one of the married men Grace Morgan had been talking about.

"Mr. Adams." The man stood and shook hands. "Have a seat."

"How's Rick's condition, Doctor?"

"Not much change, I'm afraid," the physician said.

"Are you holding out any hope for him to walk again?"

"Oh, yes," Bentley said. "I haven't given up by any means. I'm still hoping he'll walk out of here on his own."

"That's good," Clint said, "that's real good."

"Was there something else you wanted to talk to me about?" Bentley asked.

"Well, actually," Clint said, "I was hoping to speak to Jed."

"I'm sure you can find him at work—"

"I was hoping to speak to him without his bosses knowing about it," Clint said, interrupting him.

"I see," the doctor said. "Well, I could get a message to him."

"That would be good," Clint said. "Would you have him meet me at the Red Queen Hotel, just outside of Portsmouth Square?"

"When?"

"As soon as possible," Clint said. "I'm going there straight from here, and I'll wait to hear from him."

"Fine," the doctor said. "I'll get the message to him as soon as possible."

Clint stood up and shook hands again, then left. He had an itch in the center of his back. Something was going to happen, and it was going to be soon.

THIRTY-NINE

Jake Castle opened the door to his rook and said, "Get in here."

Duffy and Breck entered the room, their boss closing the door quickly behind them.

"If you two had done your job right we wouldn't be in this mess," he said immediately.

"Hell, boss, we shot him," Breck said. "Who expected him to hang on?"

"Well, now you're gonna get it done," Castle said. "I want you to go to the hospital and finish it."

"What about Clint Adams?" Duffy asked. "Want us to take care of him?"

"Clint Adams?" Castle asked. "Are you crazy? He'd chew the two of you up without breaking a sweat. Don't worry about Adams. I've got somebody else coming in to take care of him."

"Who?" Duffy asked.

Castle regarded the two men, then thought, why not?

"Reverend Jim."

"Whoa!" Breck said.

"I'd pay money to see that," Duffy said.

"Yeah, well, you're gettin' paid to do something else," Castle said. "So get to it."

"When do you want it done, boss?" Duffy asked.

"I want to wake up tomorrow and find it done, so you've got all day today."

"We'll do it, boss."

"You better," Castle said, "because if I have to have the Reverend Jim do your jobs, I'll have him take care of you, as well."

Both men swallowed hard and left the room.

In the lobby Duffy and Breck saw Clint Adams coming into the hotel from outside.

"We could take him now," Breck said.

"You're an idiot," Duffy said. "I'm not looking to face him, or the Reverend Jim. Let's just do our job, get paid, and stay alive to spend the money."

"Yeah, okay," Breck said. "You're probably right. I tell you what, though, I'd sure like to see Adams and the Reverend go at it. Where would you put your money?"

"My money stays in my pocket, where it belongs," Duffy said. "You want to waste your money on gambling, you go ahead."

"You just ain't a gamblin' man, are you?"

"Only with my life, Marty," Duffy said. "To me that's a big enough gamble."

FORTY

Clint had his choice of waiting for Jed Bentley in his room, the saloon, or the casino. He chose to wait over a mug of beer, and was seated at a table when Joe Reno showed up instead.

"What brings you here?" he asked as Reno approached his table. "I was going to come looking for you in a little while."

Reno sat down opposite Clint and said, "I got word that Reverend Jim is in the Bucket of Blood."

"Now?"

"As of an hour ago, yeah."

"Get yourself a beer, Joe."

"Aren't you going to go over there?"

"Get a beer," Clint said, "and we'll talk about it."

As Reno was at the bar getting himself a beer, Jed Bentley walked in, spotted Clint, and crossed the room to his table. He was not in uniform, and was wearing a Colt on his hip. Reno turned and Clint held three fingers up to him, meaning, "Bring three more beers."

"Mr. Adams, I got a message from my father that you needed to speak with me," Jed said.

"Have a seat, Jed," Clint said. "Let's wait for Joe Reno to join us."

"Reno?"

Jed looked up as Reno arrived with the three beers. He set them on the table and sat down.

"Jed Bentley, Joe Reno," Clint said. "Joe, Jed is a policeman."

"Is that a fact?"

"And Jed, Joe is—"

"I know who Reno is."

"—working for me, is what I was going to say."

Reno and Jed sized each other up.

"Okay, look, you fellas need to forget what side of the law you're on," Clint said. "Joe works for me, and Jed, you offered me your help. Is that offer still good?"

"Yes, sir."

"Then Joe, meet Jed."

The two young men eyed each other for a moment, then shook hands.

"Fine," Clint said, pushing a mug of beer toward each of them. "Joe, tell Jed what you just told me."

"Reverend Jim was seen in the Bucket of Blood Saloon on the Barbary Coast about an hour ago."

Jed looked at Clint, as if asking for a translation.

"Reverend Jim is this fast-rising gunman, apparently," Clint said. "I'd heard of him, but Joe had to remind me."

"Central City, a few years ago," Reno said.

"Wait," Jed said, "I know that story. Five men, right?"

"Seven," Reno said, "and I was there. They did it standing in the street, no cover, and it was over fast."

"And he's in town?"

"That's right."

"Joe feels that the only reason the Reverend would be here is for me."

"You know of anyone else in town that would warrant a gun like Reverend Jim?" Reno asked Jed.

"No, we haven't gotten any word of anyone in town with the kind of reputation Mr. Adams has. Wait, do you think Reverend Jim shot Mr. Hartman?"

"No, I don't," Clint said. "I think somebody a whole lot cheaper was paid for that, and they still might try to go to the hospital to finish the job. That's why I need you, Jed."

"What do you want me to do?"

"I want you to go to the hospital in Joe's place and relieve Andy Stryker."

"And what are you going to have . . . Joe do?"

"He's going to watch my back."

"I can do that," the young policeman insisted.

"Can you handle that hog leg on your hip, Jed?" Clint asked.

Jed hesitated, then said, "I can hit what I aim at."

"No, I mean can you handle it?"

Jed knew what he meant.

"No," he said, honestly. "I'm no gunman."

"I need to trust my back to someone who can handle a gun," Clint said, "and Joe was recommended to me by a very close friend, whose opinion I trust."

Jed nodded and said, "All right, sir, I understand."

"Jed," Clint said, "I'm trusting you with the life of a very good friend of mine."

"I know, sir," Jed said. "You can trust me."

"I know I can. I've already told Stryker to expect you. In fact, I'd even go over early, now, so the two of you overlap. I've got the feeling this thing is coming to a head."

"I'll get over there right now." He stood up.

"And Jed?"

"Yes, sir?"

"Try to forget what side of the law you and Stryker are on, just for a little while."

"I'll try, sir."

Jed nodded to Joe Reno, who returned it, and left the saloon.

"So you're taking me up on my offer to watch your back?" Reno asked.

"Yes, I am," Clint said. "I'm not about to take chances with a man like Reverend Jim."

"So are we headed for the Bucket of Blood?"

"No," Clint said, "we're going to sit here, finish our beers, and talk a bit."

"What's that going to accomplish?"

"I guess we'll find out."

FORTY-ONE

"My problem is here," Clint said to Reno, "not at the Bucket of Blood."

"But Reverend Jim—"

"If he comes here," Clint said, "then he'll become my problem. Right now my problem is Jake Castle and the banker, Ed O'Brien."

"What about them?"

"They've apparently formed a partnership," Clint said. "That's not good for anyone. Also, Wayne Jackson is gone."

"Translate all that for me," Reno said.

"Of the other three potential buyers," Clint said, "one has left town, and the other two have joined forces."

"What does that tell you?"

"That whichever one had Rick shot, the other one has aligned themselves with him."

"What if neither of them had him shot?"

"Then I'd be very surprised," Clint said. "I've looked into jealous boyfriends, but Grace Morgan only sees married men—other than Rick, that is."

"Married men can get jealous."

"A married man would not do anything to endanger his

lifestyle," Clint said. "No, it was either Castle, or O'Brien, and my money's on Castle. It's his style. If the banker thinks he's become partners with Castle, he's in for a rude awakening. Jake will turn on him in a minute."

"Seems to me if something's going to happen, it's going to happen at the hospital."

Clint thought a moment.

"If Castle and O'Brien have joined forces, then with Jackson gone Rick is the only other buyer—except he's ready to pull out."

"Is he?"

"He told me that this morning."

"But these other men don't know that."

"And neither does Grace Morgan."

"Somebody should tell them."

"I think you're right, Joe," Clint said, pushing back his chair. "Come on."

Reno stood and followed Clint out of the bar.

"How are we going to know where they are?" he asked.

"All we have to do," Clint said explained, "is put the question to the right person."

Clint and Reno approached the front desk, where Jason was still on duty.

"Can I help you, Mr. Adams?"

"Jason, I have a bet with Mr. Reno here."

"Well, sir," Jason said, "you're certainly in the right place to make a wager."

"I bet Mr. Reno here that you know the location of everyone in the hotel," Clint said. "Everyone who is anyone, that is."

"That's entirely possible."

"Where is Miss Morgan?"

"In her office."

"And Mr. O'Brien?"

"In his room."

"And Mr. Castle?"

Jason hesitated.

"You're going to make me lose my bet, Jason."

"Mr. Castle is particular about who knows his whereabouts, sir," Jason said.

Clint leaned on the desk.

"Jason, I'm not going to give you any money for Mr. Castle's whereabouts," he said, "I'm just going to tell you that I think he was behind the shooting of my friend. If I'm right, then I'm going to make him pay for it, and I'll also take it out on anyone who tries to help him."

Jason swallowed and said, "Mr. Castle is in Miss Morgan's office with her."

Clint looked at Reno and said, "Perfect."

"So what you are telling me," Grace Morgan said to Jake Castle, "is that Wayne Jackson and Rick Hartman are out of the running, and you and Mr. O'Brien have formed a partnership, so my only recourse is to sell my hotel to you?"

"That's exactly what I'm telling you."

"And are you also threatening me," she asked, "or is it just because you are a thug from New York that I think you're threatening me?"

Castle smiled instead of getting insulted. As a younger man he had been much more hotheaded, and had reacted to insults very badly. Even a woman would have had to pay for it. But this was the new Jake Castle.

"Miss Morgan," he said, "I'm not threatening you at all. I'm just telling you that I am the only option you have left if you really want to sell your hotel."

"And what about Mr. O'Brien?" she asked. "Shouldn't you have said 'we' are your only option?"

"I always say what I mean, Miss Morgan," he said.

FORTY-TWO

When Clint opened the door both Grace Morgan and Jake Castle looked up at him from their seats.

"Don't you knock, Adams?" Castle asked. "Miss Morgan and I are having a business meeting."

Reno came into the room behind Clint, closed the door, and stood in front of it.

"What's he been telling you, Grace?"

"He said that Wayne Jackson withdrew his offer on the hotel and left."

"Well, that much is true."

"He also told me that O'Brien and he are partners, and theirs is the last offer I'll get."

"That's not quite true," Clint said. Although it was, actually, Castle didn't know that Rick was going to withdraw his offer and go back to Texas. That meant he was either lying or he'd already arranged for another attempt on Rick.

"Castle," Clint said, "I've decided you're the one who had Rick shot, to get him out of the way."

"You've decided?" Castle asked, laughing. "You'll have a hard time getting the law to act on your decision, Adams."

"I don't care about the law," Clint said. "I'm going to be my own law, here." He turned to Reno. "Keep them here."

"Both of them?"

"Yes."

"And where are you off to?" Castle asked.

"The hospital," Clint said. "I think you sent your men over there to finish Rick off. I'm going to keep one of them alive to give you up, and when he does I'm coming back here for you."

"Why keep me here with him?" Grace complained.

"It's tidier," Clint said. "If either if them tries to leave, shoot them, but don't kill them."

"Got it."

Clint walked over to Castle, jerked his jacket aside, and removed his gun from his shoulder rig. He checked him for a hideout gun and didn't find one. As a last thought he walked around behind her desk and checked the drawers. He took a little pepperbox derringer from one and pocketed it.

"Remember what I said," he told Reno. "Don't kill anybody unless you have to."

"I'll remember."

"I'll see you both back here in a little while."

"Good luck, Adams," Castle said.

"You better hope I don't have any," Clint told him.

FORTY-THREE

When Jed Bentley arrived at the hospital he went to see his father first before checking in at Rick Hartman's room with Stryker.

That was his first mistake.

Duffy and Breck discussed the matter and decided they would take extra help with them to the hospital. Duffy knew some men, so they made a detour to pick three of them up.

That was their first mistake.

Andy Stryker was sitting in a chair in Rick's room with his back against the door.

"Jesus, Stryker, at least come over here where I can see you when we talk," Rick complained.

"That's okay, Rick," Stryker said, "I'm comfortable right here."

Andy Stryker didn't make mistakes.

When Duffy, Breck, and the three men they'd hired for the day reached the hospital, Jed Bentley was still in with his father. Father and son were discussing whether or not

175

Jed was compromising his principles by working with men like Joe Reno and Andy Stryker.

The five men entered the hospital, startling the nurse on the front desk.

"Excuse me," she said, leaving her station to confront them. She was an imposing woman with thick hips and legs, and she would have probably intimidated one man, or two—but not five men with guns.

"What room is Hartman in?" Duffy demanded.

"Hartman?" she asked. "Rick Hartman?"

"That's right."

She glared at the five men and asked, "Who are you?"

Duffy smiled and said, "We're his cousins."

She gave them a dubious look and said, "You don't resemble him at all—or each other."

Suddenly, Duffy drew his gun, which was the signal to the other four men to do the same. The nurse saw five gun barrels pointing at her, and they all looked the same—dark and dangerous.

"Oh, my," she said.

"Hartman."

She pointed a shaky finger down the hall and said, "Room Fourteen."

"Thanks," Duffy said. "Now go behind that desk and stay there."

"Y-yes sir."

As she ran to her desk and crouched down behind it Duffy said, "Let's go."

Leaning back against the door Stryker thought he could feel something, like the vibrations of someone walking—more than one man walking, almost marching through the halls.

"Rick."

"What?"

"Don't move."

"Very funny."

Stryker's instincts told him to stay right where he was.

Duffy saw the door with the number fourteen on it and stopped walking.

"There it is," he said. "He's bound to have someone in there with him, maybe even a policeman."

"Good," one of the other men said, "we get to kill a lawman."

"We kill anyone in that room," Breck said. "Everyone . . . right?"

"Everyone," Duffy said. "I'll go first."

He approached the door . . .

"All right, Father," Jed Bentley said, getting up from his chair, "I guess I'd better get going."

"Look at it as an adventure, Jed," Dr. Bentley said. "How often will you get a chance to assist someone like Clint Adams?"

"Never," Jed said, "or so I thought."

He left his father's office and walked toward the front entrance. He'd have to go past the reception desk in order to go down the hall to Rick's room. As he passed it he saw that it was empty, but he heard someone breathing, almost gasping, behind it. He walked over and saw the nurse crouching behind it.

"Nurse, what happened?"

She looked up at him with wide eyes and said, "Men . . . guns . . ."

"Men . . . where?"

At that moment he heard a sound from down the hall, in the direction of Rick Hartman's room, and then the first shot.

Clint paid the cab driver and then ran up the front steps to the front door of the hospital. He'd almost reached the door when he heard the first shot as well.

• • •

Remaining in the chair, leaning against the door, Andy Stryker probably saved the lives of both Rick Hartman and himself. When Duffy tried to open it with one shove it didn't budge. It helped that Stryker's chair was up on two legs. It was as if he had jammed it beneath the doorknob. When the first kick came, it even resisted that—but it was time to move.

He threw himself from the chair just as the first shot came. The bullet punched through the door and imbedded itself in the wall above Rick's head.

Stryker drew his gun and kicked the chair away from the door.

Jed Bentley rushed headlong into the hallway with his gun drawn, saw the men outside the door, and shouted, "Halt! Police!"

That was his second mistake!

As Clint entered the lobby, gun drawn, he watched as five men bunched down the hall in front of Rick's room turned and fired. At least two bullets struck the young policeman, three missed—two of those barely missing Clint and shattering the glass in the door behind him.

"Jed!"

Jed Bentley fell onto his back, his gun skittering across the floor. It came to a stop at the feet of his father, who had rushed out to see what was happening.

"Jed?" he called.

"Stay back!" Clint shouted.

He ran to the fallen young man to shield him from any other harm. He crouched in front of him and fired at the armed men.

Duffy said to Breck, "We go into the room. The rest of you take care of them."

The three men turned to obey, while Duffy and Breck rushed the door together, slamming into it with their shoulders. But since there was no resistance now, they went flying through it much faster than they had anticipated.

As the door flew open and the two men came stumbling through, Stryker regained his feet and fired. His first shot struck Breck in the side. The man cried out, fell to the floor, his gun jarred from his hand. His second shot missed Duffy because he hit the bed and went sprawling onto it. He turned, though, immediately and pointed his gun at Stryker, who saw the move and threw himself onto the floor just as Duffy pulled the trigger.

However, the move entangled him with Breck, who was wounded, but not dead. The man immediately wrapped his arms around Stryker, in an attempt to hold him for his partner . . .

Clint's first shot took one of the men in the chest. The others dropped to the floor and fired back, but their hurried shots went wild.

Suddenly, the doctor was at his side.

"Take him," Clint said.

Doctor Robert Bentley grabbed his wounded son beneath the arm and dragged him from the line of fire.

There was no cover in the hallway. The two men on their bellies realized this and stood up. Clint rose from his own crouch, and they faced each other.

"There are two of us," one of them shouted.

"There were three," Clint said. "Think about that."

The three of them stood with their guns held at their sides, facing each other.

"Okay, okay," one of them said, "let us pass."

"Drop your guns, and then you can go."

The two men looked at each other, and then down at their dead friend.

"Okay, okay," they said, again.

They started to bend their knees, reaching to put their guns on the floor, but at the last moment they brought the guns to bear on Clint, who was ready for the move.

He brought his own gun up and fired twice before either man—day-hired guns—could pull their triggers . . .

Stryker fought against Breck, but the man was strong and desperate. Duffy got off the bed and stood over both fallen men. Slowly, Stryker could feel the life draining from the dying man, but it wouldn't be soon enough. He couldn't free his gunhand from the man's grasp.

"Sorry, friend," Duffy said.

He was about to pull the trigger when there was a shot from another quarter. The bullet struck him in the throat. A torrent of blood gushed from his mouth and he fell forward, on top of Stryker and the dying Breck. Seconds later Stryker extricated himself from the two dead men and stood up. In the corner of the room, crouched and holding Breck's gun out ahead of him was Rick Hartman.

Clint ran down the hall, leaping over the dead men, and rushed into the hospital room.

"Rick!"

He stopped when he saw Stryker standing over two dead men, and Rick Hartman standing in the corner on his own two feet, holding a gun.

"I'm all right, Clint," Rick said, as shocked as anyone in the room. "I'm all right."

FORTY-FOUR

Clint awoke with that warm, firm hip pressed against him again. He was getting used to it, after seven days.

Brandy woke and stretched next to him.

"Is this the day you're leaving?" she asked.

"Yes."

"Really?"

He'd tried to leave several times before, but this time he was going to make it.

"Yes."

She smiled and said, "Then I can't let you leave without a big good-bye."

She rolled over, mounted him, and rode him while dangling both of her big good-byes in his face. . . .

He was going to miss Brandy. Not only her body and boundless energy in bed, but her personality, as well. Luckily, Rick had agreed to keep her on, along with most of the other employees—including Jason. He was, in fact, promoted by Rick to manager, as Rick still planned to spend most of his time in Labyrinth—as soon as he was able to travel. Clint told him he'd see him in Labyrinth in a couple of months.

He came down to the lobby with his saddlebags, having said good-bye to Rick the night before. His friend had moved into what used to be Grace Morgan's room, the largest in the hotel. Grace had left as soon as she and Rick signed the papers to finalize the sale. Once he was able to stand again, Rick had decided to go ahead and buy the Red Queen. He had not decided, yet, whether to rename it or not.

Things had a way of working out, Clint thought. Jed Bentley had survived his wounds, thanks to his father, the excellent doctor. Rick had been able to move from the hospital to the hotel three days ago, once he was the full owner. Brandy was going to be working there, and Jason, and Clint felt he had another place to hang his hat, now, whenever he felt the need. Of course, things had a way of changing, too, but only time would tell what the final outcome would be.

The only thing that made him angry was that Rick had persuaded him not to kill Jake Castle. Since Clint had not been able to take either Duffy or Breck alive, he hadn't been able to have them name Castle as the man who hired them. When he returned to the hotel the day after the shooting he'd found Joe Reno right where he left him, keeping Castle and Grace in her office.

"Let him go," he'd said.

"What?" Reno was shocked, but did as he was told.

Castle had walked past both men, looked at Clint, and said, "Another time, perhaps."

"Another time, definitely," Clint had said.

Castle checked out that day, and hadn't been seen since.

In the lobby he found Joe Reno and Andy Stryker waiting. They had both been offered jobs by Rick, and were now jointly running what would become the security staff of the hotel.

"You fellas seeing me off?"

"It's our job to make sure troublemakers leave the hotel, and town," Reno said.

Clint shook hands with both men and wished them luck.

"You know," Clint asked, "I wonder what happened to the Reverend Jim?"

"I heard he saved a lot of souls down at the Bucket of Blood," Reno said.

"I get the feeling you and he will cross paths eventually, Clint," Stryker said. "It's got to happen."

"Maybe," Clint said, "or maybe we'll just keep traveling in different circles."

As Clint rode Duke out of the livery stable and down the street in the direction of the railroad station, a man in a black duster and black flat-brimmed hat watched him from across the street. Reverend Jim had never heard from Jake Castle again, and had spent most of his time in San Francisco saving sinners on the docks. He did, however, from time to time, come to sneak a peek at the man known as the Gunsmith. It would have been interesting, going up against him, saving his soul and releasing it to the heavens. It wasn't something he would do for free, though.

He struck a match, lit a cigarette, and started walking down the street. Another time, maybe.

Another time, definitely.

Watch for

NO TURNING BACK

267th novel in the exciting GUNSMITH series
from Jove.

Coming in March!

J. R. ROBERTS
THE
GUNSMITH

JAKE LOGAN
TODAY'S HOTTEST ACTION WESTERN!

Explore the exciting Old West with one of the men who made it wild!

WILDGUN

THE HARD-DRIVING WESTERN SERIES
FROM THE CREATORS OF *LONGARM*

Jack Hanson